FALLING FOR THE MAD KING

FALLING
FOR THE
MAD KING

TO WIN A DARK HEART

SYDNEY WINWARD

Falling for the Mad King

Cover Art by MoorBooks Design

Published by Silver Forge Books
Paperback ISBN 978-1-960461-29-2
Digital ISBN 978-1-960461-25-4
www.sydneywinward.com

For my daughter who loves fairy tales and pointed out that I love the villains. She's right.

BOOKS BY SYDNEY WINWARD

The Bloodborn Series

Bloodborn

Bloodbond

Bloodscourge

Bloodbane

Bloodcurse

Bloodheir

Letters to Love Series

Yours, Sterling

Forever, Mirabelle

Always, Ivette

Charles, With Love

Adoringly, Edward

Sunlight and Shadows Series

A Breath of Sunlight

A Taste of Shadows

A Glimpse of Music

A Kiss of Embers

A Balm of Healing

A Weave of Starlight

Stand-Alones

Venom Kissed

Through Wylder Meadows

Root Brew Float

On Silver Wings

Bloodmoon

Selkie

A Wingless Hope

Taken by the Ripper

Falling for the Mad King

A Most Unfortunate Birthday

Nothing good ever came of blindfolds, King Rylan Rhapsody's mother once said.

His great grandfather had worn a blindfold moments before getting attacked by the Jabberwocky. His sister had worn a blindfold at a party before getting pushed into the river of memories and was never seen again. His own father? That's right. He'd lost a duel due to his hubris after claiming he could win in a sword fight with both eyes closed.

Always keep your eyes wide open, she'd often cautioned.

But Rylan wasn't always one to heed wise counsel. He felt invincible wearing a blindfold as his best friend led him by a rope deeper into the forest judging by the singing flowers to his left and the sweet nectar scent of the blooming mushrooms somewhere to his right.

"We're almost there," Alice said breathlessly, the slack on the rope tightening with each step through the whimsical terrain.

Oh, how he adored surprises. Moreso when he failed at correctly guessing the surprise. Unfortunately, today was not such a day.

He pushed his large, black curls away from his forehead and grinned at his friend, feigning ignorance. "Give me a hint. Just a little one."

"You'll see soon."

Several moments later, they stopped in a quiet, peaceful area filled with his favorite jubjub birds squawking high in the boughs above him. The ravenous fowls loved a good meal to chase, and the danger they posed was thrilling. He'd caught one once, and it currently lived as a beautiful centerpiece in his bedroom back at the castle.

A tugging sensation pulled at the back of his head as Alice untied the blindfold. His golden eyes momentarily struggled against the transition from darkness to light, but finally his surroundings came into focus.

A long, rectangular table laden with rows of pies, tarts, pastries, teacups, plates, and more stared back at him, surrounded by some of his closest friends. Gideon Glimmer with his tall hat and monocle magnifying the size of one of his ebony eyes. Julian Jester wearing a hundred rings between eleven fingers. Luna Larkspur with a body made of branches rather than skin and bones. Piper Pixiefoot and her iridescent wings fluttering at her back. Only to name a few.

"Surprise!" they all shouted in chorus, throwing confetti into the air. "Happy unbirthday!"

Rylan's hand flew to his heart as he feigned surprise. "But it was my unbirthday last month!" he laughed, shaking his head. "You shouldn't have."

"You adore unbirthdays," Alice contradicted with a hand on her hip.

"It's true. I do." He sat down at the head of the table with a flourish of his arms, his heart crown lopsided on top of his head. His friends followed suit, each passing dishes around with a cacophony of clattering porcelain and laughing grins.

He could never pass up an unbirthday celebration, but in the back of his mind, he couldn't help but review everything he needed to do back home. Oversee his rose garden. Collect taxes to construct the sky bridge over the palace. Arrange a marriage between two nobles who could better support his position as King.

Oh, and there was that man he'd placed in the gibbet yesterday…

He grimaced, realizing he'd forgotten about him. He'd only wanted to make him an example for mocking his outfit. Perhaps he might stop by sometime today and poke him with a stick to find out if he was still alive.

"Guards, Rylan?" Alice jested, nodding her head somewhere behind him. "You can't leave them behind even once?"

He turned to find half of the six palace guards dressed in black with gold buttons and white capes and the other three dressed in white with gold buttons and red capes. Each held a spear in their hands and stood at attention with black helmets covering the top half of their heads and shadowing their eyes from view.

"Not even once. A king never knows when he might need them." He shook his head and turned back to the table to find Alice sifting fluffy sugar over his pastries like the snow he'd only heard of existing in the upper world.

Occasionally, people from the upper world found their way to the Mad Lands. Usually exiled crazies or people who had fallen too far down the rabbit hole. But to visit the foreign world himself? The idea discomforted him almost as much as the thought of not a single unbirthday in an entire year. How would he manage in a world with beasts called dogs, a sun that rose by itself rather than plucked out of the sky by a giant, and an earth that grew nonsense called potatoes and rye? It was not a place he desired to visit.

Alice sat cross-legged on the edge of the table, her attention preoccupied by Felix Flamewood, a half-man, half-caterpillar who held a book in two hands, used utensils in another two hands, smoked a pipe, and blew his nose into a handkerchief with another hand. Apparently, he was allergic to Wonderland's whimsical air. More than once, he'd talked about finding a way to the upper world to escape this atmosphere, but he'd mused he'd likely be attacked on sight by men with sharp teeth and pointy swords.

After taking another bite of his rackleberry tart, he coughed as if *he* were also allergic to the air. Perhaps Felix was onto something...

Rylan swallowed, finding the action difficult after consuming so many tea tarts and pocket pies. He reached for his cup a second time and took a long swig of pumpernickel tea. He coughed, pounding twice on his chest as if something had lodged itself inside.

A prickling sensation traveled from his fingertips, up his arms, and gathered below his collarbones as his insides seemed to grow heavier with each passing moment.

His vision tipped one way and then the other until his surroundings twisted like the inside of a kaleidoscope, blurring with a cacophony of colors and strange sensations.

Alarm flitted through him when he recognized the bitter scent of magic and chaos. Lifting a hand, he tried to call for aid from one of his guards, but his fingers warped as if snatched by a pool of fairy dust and spinning through colorful skies.

Through his hazy vision, he barely gathered someone in a short blue dress skipping across the table, shattering dinnerware and smashing pastries with each footfall. Moments later, Alice's blurry face entered his vision. But rather than a warmth in her blue eyes, only coldness stared back at him.

She lifted an arm, revealing the metallic, fingerless glove she wore on her right hand. "The tyranny of the King of Hearts ends today," she hissed.

Rylan tried to leap backward, but all he managed was to sway through his dizziness until he tripped on his own foot and sat back in his chair with a thud. Panic consumed him when her glove lit up with a magical eerie red glow, and before he managed to cry out or plead, she plunged her entire hand directly into his chest.

He gasped as an unforgiving chill shot through him like a bolt of lightning striking the surface of a raging sea. Time seemed to stop as he stared disbelievingly at the unnatural way her hand disappeared inside his body. But his shock only lasted so long before she ripped her hand back out, taking his heart with it.

A scream of agony tore from his mouth. His vision darkened until he found himself no longer able to focus on anything but the blinding pain and the shock of the situation.

The darkness dispersed just enough to catch a glimpse of the heart she held in her hand. A sparkling red crystal fluctuated with a pulsing light. Alive but no longer beating inside his chest. With that heart, she could do so much damage to his reign. She held the power to rule Wonderland within her fingers.

Anger replaced his shock as he pushed himself to his feet through his dizziness and drew his sword. But rather than a weapon made of metal, it decided to transform into a winged serpent, throwing its large, lazy body across the tea table. It wouldn't do much damage, but it didn't have to. Snakes were Alice's worst fear.

She screamed at the sight of the serpent, nearly dropping his heart in the process of stuffing it inside a bag. Turning on her heel, she bolted in the opposite direction, her blonde hair flying in the wake of her flight.

"Guards, catch her!" Rylan shouted, holding one hand to his burning chest and the other scrambling to pull himself along the edge of the table, where the other guests ducked beneath to cower away from the serpent. His feet struggled to brace against the ground when his body felt weak and his mind continued to spin with dizziness.

The guards dressed in black, red, and gold had already started to rush forward before he'd called for their aid, weapons drawn. He tried to follow them but only managed two steps before his body collapsed on him.

His hands and knees hit the soft earth with a thump, his head continuing to spin through whatever poisonous substance Alice had likely put in his tea. He gritted his teeth, struggling to remain conscious.

Alice had his heart. He needed it back!

However, his body refused to obey him when he ordered his legs to stand, for his hands to push himself to his feet. The battle for consciousness lost as he fell onto his side, his eyes staring blearily at the friends who continued to huddle fearfully beneath the table.

And then darkness crashed over him like a giant pulling the shades of night over the sky.

He wasn't aware of how much time had passed in his unconscious state, only that he awoke sometime later to the sweet scent of roses and a honey nectar upon his lips.

He blinked slowly as confusion won over any attempt to recall how he had ended up in his bedchambers. Several bouquets of roses ranging from red to pink, from gold to black, filled his room. Anger coursed through him at the sight of them. No one was allowed to touch his roses, no matter the occasion, aside from the gardener. Whoever had cut his beautiful flowers would pay for their actions. The deed would not go unpunished, but it was the least of his concerns at the moment.

Little by little, his surroundings came more into focus. The golden embellishments on the arches above him. The fanciful mushroom embroidery on the sheets. The golden-brown jubjub bird biting at the bars of its cage in the middle of the room.

And then the guards standing at the foot of the bed with their spears pointed toward the ceiling. They shook with fear, quaking in their boots as they bowed to him several times.

Finally, Rylan's memory returned enough for him to recall the tea party and his best friend's cruel deception. He struck out at his table with a fist, one of the two vases tipping precariously before falling over the edge and crashing to the floor in a heap of broken petals and shattered glass.

"Where is she?" he thundered. "Where is Alice?"

"W-w-we didn't catch her, sire," one of the men stuttered. "We're unbelievably sorry."

"Yes, so sorry," the other echoed.

Rylan reached for the second bouquet of roses sitting on the table beside him and grabbed the yellow rose. He closed his fist around the stem tightly, his hand shaking with the fury growing inside him like a disease. The thorns pricked into his skin, blood dripping down his hand and soaking into the hem of his white sleeve.

What a lovely color. He fancied red.

Tipping the rose toward his face, he inhaled its sweet fragrance, sucking out the magic within to mold with his own fingertips, before turning his glare toward his guards. "Let's find out just how sorry you are."

In tandem, the guards screamed, clutching their heads as Rylan assaulted them with illusions of dark caverns and blood-thirsty monsters. Each fell to the floor in a fetal position, their screams hardly doing justice to the anger burning through his now heartless chest.

His best friend had betrayed him.

He would make sure she regretted the day she had ever set foot in the Mad Lands.

ONE CURSE TOO MANY

Many people thought immortality was a blessing. Something to strive for. Something to *obsess* over. Those people had never had their hearts broken.

Ellie Strife stood outside the castle wall, gazing somberly into a tall, floor-to-ceiling glass window as the rain roared down from the skies and pelted the dark purple cloak she wore to conceal her identity. The water quickly soaked into the fabric and next into her curly auburn hair until the strands lay flat, deflated, and frizzy against the slick texture of her neck.

She placed a hand on the glass, the warmth from her fingers contrasting against the cool surface and fogging up the window.

Men and women danced across the large ballroom, the enormous chandeliers casting light on the party guests within. Twelve little princesses ranging from ages six to twenty laughed and smiled as they danced together in a circle with the eldest—the bride—in the middle with her new husband, the wretched man who had broken Ellie's midnight dancing curse. They'd deserved their fate after...after...

Pain broke out across her jaw when she clenched her teeth too hard. Her steaming glare fixed on the man responsible for her hurt, for her pain.

King Melgren sat on his silver throne as he watched his daughters dance, a glittering crown of green jewels sitting atop his head. He was older now. Much older. Silver streaked across once brown hair, wrinkles set in the folds of his skin. Hands once fresh and youthful now sported brown spots and jutting veins.

How much time had passed? Fifty years?

Yet, she still looked the same as the day he'd declared his undying love for her and promised to run away with her, only to jilt her and marry another the very next day.

The best way to strike at someone was to hit them where it hurt the most. Ellie had once planned to steal away his son, his heir, but his wife had born only daughters. Those daughters had deserved her curse, if only to hurt the man who had shattered her heart and stained it black.

She felt it now within her. A weak, disjointed rhythm. A heaviness only a tainted black heart could carry.

Her fist closed against the glass, the tips of her knuckles dripping with frigid rain. If King Melgen wanted to witness his daughter's joy so badly, then that was exactly what she'd give him. To live the same day repeatedly. To laugh until it rubbed one's throat raw. To dance until one's feet bled with blisters. To watch a wedding again and again and again until the vows were permanently inscribed in one's brain.

To never watch one's children grow older…

King Melgren needed to answer for what he'd done, for the life and love he'd stolen from her.

Ellie lifted her hand, a silver mist threading around her fingers like moonlight thread. A strong sense of injustice enveloped her, a desire for unanswered punishment overwhelming her thoughts.

But just like the first time she'd tried to curse Melgren and his daughters, her magic flickered out when the type and longevity of the curse proved too much. She needed something stronger to fuel the curse.

Love.

She needed a heart.

More specifically, she needed *his* heart.

She nearly scoffed at the idea. The man was incapable of love. Leaving her as he had without a single apology or explanation. Just…nothing.

Inside, the king laughed and clapped his hands as one of his younger daughters performed a merry jig. His smile… His laugh… The *happiness* in his eyes. He did not deserve it. The injustice of his happiness pricked her like a thorny bracelet constricting around her heart with each shallow breath.

The sopping fabric of her cloak slapped against her skirts as she spun around and walked briskly toward the servant's entrance of the palace. No, she didn't quite look the part of subservient maid, nor did she quite fit the mold of the nobles dancing inside.

Something in between. She would stand out. But she no longer cared about her own fate as long as she found retribution.

As she strode through narrow hallways around bustling servants and platters filled with food and drinks, silver magic wove around her, pulling the water from her hair and clothing until her auburn curls bounced lightly with each step, and the dark burgundy of her skirts shifted freely without the heavy weight of water dragging them down.

Several servants cried out in fright. One of them dropped a metal platter, and it clattered to the ground with a deafening echo, followed by a variety of cheeses scattering across the floor. None of them should recognize her, but she reckoned they feared the magic of a sorceress.

Ellie hissed through her teeth and pretended to lunge forward at one of the servants. The woman cried out and sank to her knees, her hands held together in a pleading gesture.

With an amused grin, she continued down the hallway, servants parting for her like stiff grass beneath a lioness's paws.

On her way, she snapped her fingers, her own purple cloak disappearing in a wisp of silver magic. Then, she snatched a servant's cloak from a hook and threw it over her shoulders. People already knew she was here. At this point, it was only a matter of getting as close to the king as possible before one of the guards noticed her presence.

Next, she snatched a platter filled with glasses of bubbling liquid from a man and ducked her head to give herself the appearance of meek servitude. If she looked someone in the eye, people might start asking questions.

After rounding several corners, she finally entered the ballroom and forced herself to keep her gaze down rather than searching for the king's location. Though, she guessed he lingered near his giggling daughters as they continued to dance through the night.

One more curse. Just one, and she would surely be free from this overwhelming feeling of injustice. Perhaps she might finally be able to move on into the next phase of her life.

She lifted her gaze the slightest bit and easily found the king dancing with his daughter, the bride, twirling her across the dance floor. Once upon a time, that could have been her dancing in his arms. That could have been her smile and her happiness. Those could have been her daughters, a big, happy family no matter if they were royalty or peasants.

"There she is!" a guard somewhere behind her hissed barely loud enough for her to hear as if not wanting to alarm the guests over her presence.

Ellie shoved the tray she held into another servant's arms and strode more purposefully toward the middle of the dance floor.

One heart. One curse. Justice brought to fruition.

King Melgren spotted her first, his eyebrows shooting upward into his gray hairline with recognition. He grabbed his daughter by the hand and pushed her behind him before positioning himself between her and Ellie.

Silver magic sparked between her fingers as she continued forward. Every fiber of her being screamed at her to beg and plead and demand answers. But after years of nothing but disdainful silence, she knew it was a lost cause. No words. Just action. It was the only way to reach through the thick skull beneath his silvery crown.

"*The happiest day, one must live,*" Ellie said as her curse flared to life, and her magic grew brighter around her. "*Again and again, the days you give. Trapped in a moment, long for a day. Until the time comes when your hearts shall decay—*"

Something slammed into her from behind. She grunted as she collapsed to her knees, her magic flickering out until the silver threads disappeared. She was left with nothing but the ringing in her ears and black dots dancing at the edges of her vision while the back of her head throbbed with an unrelenting ache.

Yet, she was not deterred.

Through the ringing in her ears, she noticed the entire room had hushed. Even the flickering candlelight seemed to hold its breath high above her. But Melgren's stunned expression screamed quietest of all.

After several unbearably long moments, someone coughed, the sound startling the stillness of the atmosphere. Only then did Melgren step forward, towering high above her. He used to be tall, but his old age had shortened his stature considerably.

"I am offended you didn't invite me to the wedding," Ellie said, speaking first with her head held high. "We used to be..." The corner of her mouth lifted in a sly smirk as she whispered, "...so close."

The king glanced back and forth as if afraid someone might have heard her, the tips of his weathered ears turning red. "You will be punished for your crimes."

"Oh? And pray do tell... What are they?"

"Cursing my beautiful daughters to dance every night until their feet became blistered, to begin with."

"You have proof?"

Melgren leaned forward and snarled, "I don't need proof. I know it was you. You have been antagonizing me for years."

Just a little closer now...

"I'm too old," she said with a bite of her lip. "I couldn't hear what you said. Come a little closer."

He leaned toward her, his nose twitching with anger. "I said—
"

Ellie lunged forward with her hand, but the moment her fingers touched the sash draped over one of his shoulders, someone grabbed her arm from behind. A searing heat burned into her skin, and she cried out at the unexpected agony.

Her eyes widened. Magic burned a black anti-magic mark into her wrist like a scorch mark left behind by witch's fire, forming the shape of a circle with several penetrating spikes.

A magic disrupting sigil.

"You knew I was coming!" she gasped, glancing from the sigil to the sorcerer behind her to the king, who wore a triumphant smirk.

"On my daughter's important day? Of course, I did. Predictable."

In a moment of desperation, she ripped her arm out of the sorcerer's grip and reached for her magic. But instead of finding a pool of power waiting for her to mold, steep walls lay around the pool, too thick and too high to penetrate or climb. Her magic was blocked. Inaccessible.

Out of reach...

Raising his voice, King Melgren pointed directly to her and spoke for everyone to hear, "Sorceress Ellie Strife, I hereby banish you to the Mad Lands! May your magic and discord never again touch the prosperous kingdom of Elyria."

All the blood and warmth rushed from Ellie's face. The Mad Lands were rumored to alter someone's mind until they became an unrecognizable shell of the person they once were. Once exiled, no one ever returned. At least not of the same mind.

"I promise you, Melgren," she hissed, her eyebrows furrowed with a glare. "If you do this, I will wreak vengeance on your prosperity like nothing you have encountered before."

The threat gave him pause, the color draining from his own face. Still, he waved his wrist to shoo her away like some sort of hungry, mangy animal. "Take her there tonight. I do not wish to see her face again."

She refused to believe her magic was inaccessible. It had been her constant companion, a gift she had practiced and honed over the two hundred and fifty years of her life. It wouldn't desert her now. Not ever.

"*Until the time comes when your hearts shall decay,*" she tried again, lifting her hand to harness her magic. "*A penance to keep—*"

Something hit her from behind for a second time, and unlike the last instance, she found herself unable to remain upright of her own free will. She slumped to the ground, the darkness finally overcoming her. Her consciousness stirred lightly when rain sprinkled her face, and then again when the whinny of a horse pulled her out of the darkness for a sliver of a moment.

At last, her body jolted awake when she landed in sloshy mud that soaked into her clothing and clung to the strands of her hair until her head became heavy from the weight.

She blinked confusedly against the onslaught of rain pelting her face and the slimy ground squishing between her fingers. The dark silhouettes of trees surrounded her, barely visible with the moon hidden behind several layers of thick, gray clouds.

Two men grabbed each side of her, dragging her to her feet. Her mind spun disorientingly with every faltering step. Where was she? How had she arrived here?

But then she spotted the large ring of redcap mushrooms surrounding an infinite hole of ebony darkness where there was no end and no beginning.

An entrance to the Mad Lands.

Panic clawed at her chest. She ripped one of her arms out of a guard's grip and punched him squarely in the jaw. The man stumbled backward, clutching a hand to his face while complete shock registered in his eyes. The surprise attack was enough for the second guard's grip to loosen. She pulled her other arm free, picked up her sopping skirts, and sprinted toward the treeline beckoning her into the safety of its dark silhouette.

But freedom was short lived as a guard tripped her with an expertly placed foot, sending her sprawling across the ground. Mud, twigs, and grass clung to her as she attempted to claw her way to her feet. The guard grabbed a hold of her foot and dragged her back toward the mushroom circle, her fingers digging into the dirt and collecting mud beneath her fingernails.

She rolled onto her back and kicked with all her might. The man stumbled backward several steps but continued to hold on tight.

"Release me!" she shouted, kicking again with her second foot. The other guard caught it mid-air, and with a strong heave, the men pulled her onto her feet, pushing her head toward the circle like someone kneeling beneath a guillotine.

A dark abyss stared back at her, a forever nothingness threatening to drag her down with shadowed, misty claws.

"I'm not the one who deserves this!" she cried, struggling but failing to free herself from their grip. "You must believe me. King Melgren—"

The guards pushed her forward, and she only managed to grasp air before she fell through the abyss, the darkness swallowing her scream on the way down.

3

DON'T TOUCH THE ROSES

Falling forever had never been on the top of Ellie's to-do list. The nothingness of the abyss caved in on her, a darkness deep enough to overwhelm her senses. Which way was up? Which way was down? When suspended in the air, her muddy hair flailing in all directions, she lost all sense of time and place, her scream swallowed up by the bottomless void.

An array of colorful lights flickered around her. First pink, then yellow, followed by blue. Shapes came into focus next. Enormous tree roots jutting from the earth. Glowing flowers reaching for her with outstretched petals. Redcap mushrooms twirling and dancing with a non-existent breeze.

And then a clock began ticking.

Each tick slammed into her like a deafening wave, filling her mind and drenching her soul in a moment of despair. Every tock burned into her head until it screamed for silence.

A moment of weightlessness held her suspended in the air before she slammed onto the ground on a soft bed of moss.

Ellie groaned as she rolled onto her back, her surroundings spinning above her. Trees. Vines. Blue lights. Mushrooms ranging in height from the length of her hand to the tallest spire of the Elyrian castle.

The bright light of day filtered through the trees high above, momentarily disorienting her. Only minutes earlier, it had been midnight. How long, exactly, had she fallen through the hole?

She pushed herself to a sitting position, frowning at her own state of disarray. Leaves and twigs tangled in her hair. Mud caked the bottom of her shoes and the hem of her gown. A layer of grime coated her skin, the dirt flaking off like some sort of terrible disease.

Something behind a cluster of tall mushrooms released an eerie shriek. Ellie jumped to her feet, invigorated by the terror spurring her pulse into a fast rhythm. Another shriek sounded somewhere to her right. She spun around, searching for the source of the sound.

The heat rushed out of her face.

Staring back at her from the shadows of the forest were a dozen pairs of yellow eyes.

One of the creatures flapped its blue wings and landed on a branch, opening its beak to reveal two rows of dagger-sharp teeth. Several more of the creatures landed beside the first, also showing their teeth to her.

Slowly, she backed up, never taking her eyes off the bird-like monsters. If they were anything like the predators back home, sudden flight might encourage them to attack.

She instinctively reached for her magic, but once again, the sigil on her wrist blocked her attempts. If only she hadn't relied so heavily on her magic, then she might have thought to arm herself with several knives and other weapons.

A stick cracked beneath her boot, and she cringed when the birds all at once cocked their heads to the side in synchronized movement.

Ellie continued to back away. If she were lucky, the creatures would lose interest.

But she was not so lucky.

One of the birds spread their wings and released a mighty shriek to the skies. The others followed suit until her ears rang from the unpleasant noise. And then the creature leaped off the branch and dove in her direction.

She screamed as she picked up her skirts and sprinted away from the creatures snapping at her with their sharp beaks, narrowly missing piercing her skin. She needed to find a way out of the forest, but as she glanced toward the sky, she couldn't find the sun to help guide her way.

Branches jutted out of the ground, attempting to trip her as if the trees had a mind of their own. Her boots slipped on loose dirt and slimy mud, but pure desperation kept her on her feet when she otherwise might have crashed to the ground in defeat.

The shrieks became louder as the birds followed her through the forest. She weaved in and out of obstacles, attempting to outmaneuver them.

A pink light within the forest lent her hope, and she increased her pace, racing with all her might toward the source. She leaped over a small stream, ducked beneath a branch, but then she yelped in surprise when the ground caved beneath her.

Air rushed from her lungs, stealing her voice in her momentary surprise as wind rushed through her hair. Her feet kicked the air before landing hard on tall, squishy grass. She stumbled forward, unable to catch her balance, and crashed onto something soft.

"Wheeeee!" a chorus of high-pitched voices sang beneath her.

Her eyes shot wide open when she noticed the softness she'd landed on wasn't moss or grass or dirt but *fur*. Several different shades of pink and orange fur.

Ellie scrambled to her feet to find small, furry creatures the size of her hand staring up at her with large eyes rippling with pink and black stripes. Relief flowed over her, especially when she realized the monster-birds no longer chased her. The adorable little fuzzy things were a welcome change in comparison.

But then little by little, the sea of creatures began rippling between pink and black, each tripling in size before turning their changing eyes to her...

And revealing their sharp, unforgiving teeth.

"For the love!" she gasped before turning on her heel and sprinting away once again. Of course, the creatures bounded after her with large bounces and hissing breaths.

Her legs threatened to give out on her. Her lungs burned from exertion. She couldn't keep going like this. She would sooner succumb to the terrifying creatures of the Mad Lands than survive another day to tell the tale.

She continued running, desperate to place as much distance between herself and the foreign creatures.

Each gasping breath tore through her lungs like fire burning through parchment. Her entire body ached, her mind exhausted. It was no wonder why those exiled to the Mad Lands rarely returned. They were likely eaten alive before sundown.

Ellie glanced over her shoulder to find the little creatures slowing as if giving up the chase. Perhaps there was hope for her yet. Perhaps—

She slammed into something hard, and all the air rushed from her body as she crashed to the ground. Her rapid, fearful breaths transitioned into a sigh of relief when she noticed two men standing above her, each dressed in what appeared to be coordinated guardsman uniforms.

Each man wore black, but one had a white cape and the other a red cape. Black helmets shrouded their eyes in shadow, but they appeared far less menacing than the creatures trying to attack her.

"Thank the starlit mountains!" she cried, turning to find that the creatures had retreated entirely. "I thought I would never find someone out here."

But it was as if her words entered one ear and exited the other when neither acknowledged her words. One of the men stooped down and grabbed her arm, his nose wrinkling when he spotted the sigil on her wrist. "Looks like we got another one. King Rhapsody will want to see her."

"Yes!" she gasped, grabbing desperately to the man's red cape. "Take me to civilization."

The guards exchanged glances filled with something between amusement and pity. But she didn't care to dissect it when she needed to get away from the terrifying creatures of the forest and somewhere a proper bath and other people existed. Surely, this king was far safer than the monstrosities lurking about in the Mad Lands.

One of the guards led at the front, the second following behind her with the sharp end of his spear pointed at her back. It wasn't a warm welcome, but it was warmer than her first introduction to this strange place.

Her weary feet guided her forward, and she was overly aware of the weapon at her back. But hope buried its seed in her chest. She'd survived the day, and that's what mattered.

Or…at least she thought it was day.

She glanced toward the sky, her brows furrowing when she spotted the sun at a different position overhead, but nowhere near the mountaintops in the distance as it probably should be. How long were days here? When would night fall?

At long last, when her legs threatened to collapse beneath her from exhaustion, the terrain changed suddenly from endless forests to plants and shrubs and beautiful gardens filled with a variety of strange foliage she had never encountered before. She wanted to stop and study her surroundings further, but the guard behind her prodded her with the opposite end of his spear.

A short time passed before they approached enormous black gates stretching high enough into the air for her to crane her neck upward. Beneath a metal arch, four guards led a man with five eyes out of the gates. A metal collar lay around his neck with several chains protruding from it. The guards each held a chain as if leading a dangerous criminal from the grounds. Either that, or to humiliate him with such a performance.

"I'm sorry, Your Highness!" the man shouted as he craned his neck to glance behind him. "I never should have cut the roses! I'll do better, I swear!"

A guard prodded the chained man in the back of the shoulder with the butt end of his spear. "Keep moving, gardener. The king has already made up his mind about your fate."

Ellie watched with wide, uncertain eyes as they passed.

The man mumbled to himself, "Don't cut the roses. Don't touch the roses. Don't breathe on the roses. Mad King. Mad King. Mad King."

Just what, exactly, was she walking into?

One of the guards pushed her shoulder as if to remind her to keep walking. For a moment, she wasn't sure if she should try to run in the opposite direction or brave the unknown lying ahead of her.

In the end, she continued forward with purposeful strides. She refused to show weakness in front of this *Mad King*. Surely, he couldn't be worse than Melgren.

They entered the gates, and Ellie's breath fled from her entirely. Standing tall before her was a beautiful white palace with golden accents along the railings, arches, and balconies. Not a single speck of dirt marred the pristine structure.

Surrounding her in the courtyard were numerous guards dressed in red, black, white, and gold, every other one in the opposite-colored uniform to create an intimidating yet dazzling pattern. Behind those guards, people stood about whispering to one another, likely commenting on the earlier spectacle. But they weren't like the people from above. They were men with enormous feline grins and pointed teeth or women with six arms and hats large enough to dwarf the elusive sun.

A hush stole over the crowd. The strange people dipped at the knee and inclined their heads. The guards tapped the ends of their spear twice against the ground and stood at attention.

Ellie's gaze followed the path of green lawn, bushes of flowers, and up a curving white staircase seemingly crafted of starlight stone.

And then her black heart stopped beating along with her faltering breath.

At the top of the staircase stood the most beautiful man she had ever seen. Black curls brushed against tan skin. Long eyelashes shadowed breathtaking golden eyes.

And when he smiled... Absolutely dazzling.

He wore a white shirt with loose sleeves beneath a black vest. A black cape draped over one of his shoulders, the hem brushing against the top of his black boots and fitted trousers. With wrist-length, black-gloved fingers, he plucked several roses from a golden vase and inhaled their fragrance with a deep sigh. He tucked the red rose into his breast pocket, returned the gold rose to the vase, and held the white rose between his fingers.

"King Rylan Rhapsody of Wonderland," a guard announced, and everyone bowed even lower.

Ellie's brows furrowed, her lips twitching with amusement. What kind of name was that?

The king's gaze swept over the courtyard before landing on her. The gold of his eyes struck her like a heated ray of sunlight, and she momentarily found herself unable to form words, let alone thoughts. She'd never seen anyone with such striking beauty. This was truly the Mad King?

Suddenly remembering her disheveled appearance, her fingers darted to her hair to pull out loose twigs tangled within the strands. But she was an unfortunate lost cause.

He studied her for several moments before speaking, "What have you brought me today?"

What not *who.* Already, she felt dehumanized.

"We found her wandering the woods," a guard answered, lifting her wrist to show off the sigil emblazoned on her skin. "A sorceress."

Rolling his eyes, he slowly descended the staircase step by step. "Sending their crazies to us again. Well, love, we're all filled up!"

He laughed maniacally, others joining in, and slinked forward one small step at a time. "What did you do?" One step. "Poison a princess?" Two steps. "Break a glass slipper?" Three steps. "Kidnap a girl and lock her in a tower?"

She ripped her shoulder out of the guard's grip and leveled him with a glare. "Curse princesses to dance every night."

He paused on the last step, his eyebrow lifted in surprise. But then he laughed and took another long, deep breath of the rose in his hands. "You sorceresses come up with the cleverest things."

Another charming smile melted the walls of distrust around her soul as he handed the white rose to her. Surprise lifted her brows as she took the flower delicately by the stem, glancing from the smooth white petals to his alluring golden eyes.

But then she hissed when a thorn on the stem pricked her finger, drawing forth blood. She placed her finger in her mouth to stop the flow, but not before a streak of red marred the beautiful white petals of the rose.

King Rylan's eyes flashed with interest. "Oh, I do love the color red."

What kind of person would say something like that? Maybe he really was as mad as the rumors said. But somehow, his beauty diminished whatever lunacy lingered in his mind. His eyes were so golden, so mesmerizing...

"Now," he murmured, "Tell me your name."

Years of caution and distrust screamed at her to lie, to protect herself. But something about his expression was disarming, and she found herself wanting to tell him the truth. "Ellie Strife."

"Ellie Strife the sorceress." He clicked his tongue. "You must have performed some extraordinary feats to end up with that mark," he gestured to the sigil on her wrist, "*and* exiled to my magnificent kingdom."

"Not so magnificent with all these beasts in the woods."

She clamped a hand over her mouth. Why had she said that? It was almost as if the words were pulled from her tongue before she could stop them.

She felt compelled to speak the truth. Was magic at play?

"No respect for our culture? Hmmm…" His eyes took on a disinterested sheen, his mouth curving downward. "Just like the rest." He produced a pair of scissors from his pocket and placed them at the base of the flower she held. "I have decided your fate." He laughed gleefully. "Guards! Off with her head." And then he snipped the top of the rose, the lifeless flower plopping to the ground at their feet.

Guards moved forward and grasped onto her arms. In a moment of frantic desperation, she cried out to him just as he turned on his heel to leave the courtyard. "No, wait!" He stopped on the third stair but didn't glance back at her. "I'm useful. I can cook. I can clean." Her mind darted to the gardener being led away in chains, and a dangerous lie popped into her head. However, when she tried to say that she was skilled at making gardens thrive, she instead said, "I have experience working in gardens."

He held up his gloved hand, and the guards released her and took a step back.

Slowly, he turned to face her, studying her with renewed interest. "What are your qualifications?"

"I am far older than I look. I have many decades of experience tending to plants and flowers and shrubs." Ha! She managed to kill plants faster than a lightning bolt striking the ground. "You have such beautiful gardens. I would hate to see them wither away."

The king cocked his head to the side to study her, his gaze sweeping from her disheveled hair to the muddied skirts of her dress. His nose crinkled, fury flashing across his expression. "I don't like your kind here. The ones that fall from the upper world."

"Or were pushed," she muttered under her breath. Louder, she said, "I won't cause any trouble, Your Majesty. I swear." She dipped at the knee and inclined her head like she'd seen the others do. She hadn't survived a fall through the rabbit hole and a deadly chase through the woods just to die now. Survive first. Figure out how to regain her magic later.

Like the crack of a whip, his expression changed from anger and distrust to something akin to glee and merriment. He clapped his hands together. "Well then! Let's see how the new gardener fares, shall we?"

A smile lingered on his face as he leaned closer until his lips nearly brushed against the shell of her ear with his whisper. "Never, and I repeat never, touch my roses without my permission. Am I clear?"

Gooseflesh raised on her arms and the back of her neck as she nodded profusely. Call him what they would—mad, loony, insane. But she knew the truth.

This man was dangerous.

"Good." He smiled and patted the air above her cheek as if touching her in any way was beneath him. "Piper Pixiewing will show you to your quarters."

A woman with glimmering wings stepped forward and motioned for her to follow. Ellie took several steps before glancing over her shoulder. King Rylan held a golden pocket watch in his hand, staring intensely at the clock face.

Despite the temporary loss of her magic, she still felt something very wrong about the Mad Lands. Something strange. Something off.

And he was at the center of it all.

4
THE BLACKEST OF HEARTS

"*P*rotect your heart at all costs*," Rylan's mother had once said, apparent wisdom he had also failed to heed. "*Should you lose it, all will be lost.*"

Rylan rubbed his hand against his chest directly over where his heart should be, now an empty chasm of despair. His father had died when he'd been small enough to fail to remember what he'd looked like. But his mother... Gone before his seventh birthday. All this time, he'd thought she'd cautioned him to never fall in love.

How stupid of him to think otherwise.

Anger seethed through him as he stared at the looking glass pointed at his partially bare chest. Alice had left no mark behind to indicate she'd stolen what lay within. But he felt its void like the absence of the sun on a cold, wintry day. He'd actually never seen snow. But he'd heard about it from the upper dwellers. Cold like ice. But he also didn't know what ice was. Frozen water, someone had said. However, he found himself unable to imagine water becoming hard in the first place.

Setting the looking glass aside on the desk in his room, he scowled as he buttoned up his shirt to hide what he wished to forget. But no amount of concealing could erase what Rylan had done.

He'd lost the Heart of Wonderland.

Fatigue shot through his body, stealing the life and energy from him. Moments later, a slow and steady rumble moved beneath his feet as Wonderland shook and trembled. His hand shot out to the wall to keep himself steady.

The rumbling lasted only seconds, but it left an imprint of dread inside his heart.

He rolled his eyes at the thought. He no longer possessed a heart. Wherever this dread clawed up from, it certainly wasn't from there.

His mother's cautionary words entered his mind again and formed a frown on his lips. Losing the Heart of Wonderland likely caused the quakes, each stronger than the last. If he didn't find it—and Alice—soon, his entire kingdom might crumble to dust.

The questions remained. Why had she taken it? And what was she planning to do with it?

Another round of burning fatigue pressed heavy on his shoulders, reminding him that without his heart, he was set on a path directly to his deathbed. He needed energy. And fast.

He pulled out his pocket watch to check the time. The numbers jumped around in their excitement to see him but finally settled long enough for him to catch the hour. Fifteen past teatime. Ugh. He'd missed his favorite meal of the day. No matter. He'd attend tomorrow instead.

A variety of roses lay within a vase on the table next to his door. The tips of his fingers skimmed over soft, colorful petals before landing on an orange, silky texture. Orange like the sunset, however infrequently they occurred in Wonderland.

He handled the flower carefully, not wanting to prick himself on a thorn. Not yet at least. But he wore gloves for that very reason. To prevent himself from getting pricked…

And to avoid touching another person.

Brushing the thoughts aside, he made his way outside into the garden, searching for his newest unwise hire. Sorcerers and sorceresses with their magic blocked only wanted one thing—to gain back their magic. This Ellie Strife would surely be no different, making her a costly liability. It would have been better for her head to receive the ax. But now wasn't the time to neglect his roses. He needed a gardener now more than ever.

After fruitlessly searching the enormous gardens for several minutes, he finally heard cursing and angry muttering in the section of the property with an unsolvable hedge maze. He always loved when his subjects dared to venture inside. He also loved when they inevitably got lost and needed a desperate rescue after several hours, or even days, of wandering, growing more frantic with each passing hour. Sometimes he enjoyed watching the struggle from the window of the palace tower.

He found the sorceress kneeling on the ground, her backside in the air while reaching for something beneath a stone bench. From this angle, he noticed she wore a new outfit provided for the staff, a loose, embroidered top tucked into a green skirt with a decorative brown hem. A brown belt cinched around her waist with a variety of pouches looped through it for her gardener tasks. He couldn't see her face from here, though he briefly wondered if it was still covered in dirt and grime.

"You! Witch!" he called.

The woman smacked her head on the bottom of the bench, cursing yet again as she struggled to push herself back out of the stone obstacle.

He crooked his finger, motioning for her to follow him. He turned quickly, not wanting to wait any longer than necessary and certainly not waiting for her to catch up with his long, determined strides.

The sound of her stumbling footsteps followed, her quick gasps telling him she fell into step a few paces behind him.

How long until *this* one started sneaking around to find something to bring back her magic? A day? A week? It was better to dispose of her kind early lest someone try to stab him. Again. Only Alice had been successful in her attempt to kill him or take the Heart of Wonderland or whatever she'd tried to do to him.

His fists clenched at the thought of his former friend. Somewhere out there, she still had his heart. He needed it back.

"Ah, here we are," he said as they stopped in front of rows upon rows of ebony roses the color of a midnight sky. He turned to face the sorceress, but his words faltered, and his breath stuttered.

Standing before him was no longer a deranged woman covered in mud, sticks, and who knew what else. Her curly auburn hair was tied behind her, reaching her lower back, while two curly strands framed either side of her face. No longer hidden beneath a layer of mud lay a spatter of freckles over her cheeks and the bridge of her nose.

And her eyes...

Dark brown like the color of a deep, rich chocolate that melted in the mouth...

Her plump pink lips lifted into a sly grin as if she'd caught him staring. Ugh. These sorceresses were all the same. The ones that lived through the fall into the forest, at least. He recalled the sorceress who had locked a poor girl in a tower her entire life. Something about long hair and kidnapped princesses.

Internally, he snapped his fingers to try to remember the woman's name. Dame Gothic, or something like that. She'd heavily flirted with him before trying to drive a dagger through his ribs. These crazies were dangerous. But that made it fun and interesting. At least until the almost dying part.

The reminder pulled him out of his thoughts long enough for him to inhale a deep breath of the orange rose in his hand, taking in its subtle magic with its tangy fragrance. Then, he held it out to her, handling it at the base of the flower so she had no choice but to take it from the stem.

Hesitantly, she accepted it, eyeing it and him with distrust and caution. "Is this the part where you order my head on the chopping block again?"

"Oooh!" He clapped his hands together. "Such a great idea. I had so much fun the last time."

She stared wide-eyed at him with a disbelieving curl to her lips as if she didn't know what, exactly, to make of him. As if she had no idea whether he was serious or ready to order her death. He wasn't sure yet himself. His current mood might tip the scale either way.

"Ouch!" she hissed, nursing one of her fingers. "These have too many thorns. Have you ever considered trimming them?"

Rylan cupped his hand around his ear. "Pardon? I must not have heard you correctly if you suggested desecrating my darling beauties."

Right on time, the magic from the orange rose allowed him the insight to peer into her thoughts and emotions. If a crazy were about to attempt to thrust a dagger into his chest, he wanted to know about it first.

However, he wasn't prepared for the burning hatred to slam into him like the fiery breath of a jabberwocky. Ellie's expression remained blank, but the hate raging within her betrayed the cool facade she painted on her face. The feeling was so intense that nothing remained in her heart for anything else, not allowing him to gain further insight into her thoughts.

Who, exactly, was her hate directed toward?

He mentally pushed her emotions away and grimaced as he flicked his hands as if the action might rid him of the taint her fire and darkness had infected him with. He had enough of that to deal with himself, and he didn't need any more, thank you very much.

Taking a step forward, his shadow towered over her with the sun now directly at his back. Rather than cowering away from him, she stood tall and met him with a defiant stare of her own.

"Listen very carefully," he said as he glanced cautiously around the garden. No one stood within sight, but one never knew if someone watched from the palace windows. "Here are your instructions. Do exactly as I say, and do not deviate from your task."

He paused, staring at her expectantly. After a few moments, she blinked in confusion.

"And those tasks are...?"

"No, no, no. First you must bow and say, 'Yes, Your Majesty.'"

More confused blinking. "You're jesting."

"Nope." He inspected his nails despite the black leather gloves covering them. "Go on."

Glee swept through him when her glower hit him at full force, but still, she dipped at the knee and murmured, "Yes, Your Majesty."

Ha! Even a sorceress could bow. He didn't need an orange rose to confirm what that told him. None of her kind would bow to him unless they thought they could gain something from subservience. Now... What did this particular witch want?

Aside from saving herself from the impending doom of losing her head, of course.

He pointed to the black roses, making sure not to turn his back to her for a single second. "I want you to cut these and place them in vases. A dozen per vase." He patted each of his pockets, trying to locate his list. But each pocket came up empty. Had he misplaced it?

"Ah! There you are!" he cried triumphantly as he slipped a rolled piece of parchment from a section of his hair. He pulled and pulled until it came free, the entire length of his arm.

Ellie stared at him incredulously, and the lingering effects from the orange rose revealed an echo of her thoughts. *"This man's a lunatic..."*

It took all his self-control not to snort and burst into laughter. Upper dwellers were all the same. Unable to adjust to a whimsical world versus one that followed all their stingy rules.

Pressing the parchment into her hand, he said, "This includes eight addresses. I want you to *hand deliver* each vase of roses to its recipient. Do not pass this task off to anyone else. Do not mistake one household for another. Only handle twelve cut roses at a time."

The sorceress's mouth pinched, her nose wrinkling as if she'd caught a whiff of something foul. "Did someone die?"

"What are you talking about?"

She gestured to the roses. "Black roses are for mourning."

"Black roses are *regal* and *beautiful* and have nothing to do with loss." Well, actually... "Do not associate them with death again."

He motioned to the ground with his eyes, enjoying watching the way she gritted her teeth and barely repressed a glare. Finally, she dipped at the knee.

"Yes, Your Majesty."

Hahaha! This was fun. He enjoyed making a sorceress squirm, however long it lasted before she decided to make an attempt on his life. The story was always the same. Once they came sniffing over the great power he wielded, they always wanted to take a bite. Or, more like an entire mouthful. Such greedy little creatures.

He turned away from her but stopped in his tracks and lifted a gloved hand over his shoulder. "And don't doze off in the rose garden. You will be punished if caught."

And not by him. The warning was with the best intentions in mind. Simply dealing with the black roses would siphon some of her energy, tempting her to take a rest. If she fell asleep while handling so many of the flowers at once, she might not wake up at all.

It was in her best interest—and his—for her to remain cautious and vigilant.

"Noted," she replied dryly.

Oh, how he enjoyed the attitude she gave him! Sorceresses were far too entertaining for their own good. Even if they *did* come from the upper world.

With purposeful strides, he entered the castle with the intention of getting back to work, but two guards approached bowing, each quaking and shaking in their boots.

"No sign of Alice, sire!" one of them said, now bowing low enough for his long hair to brush against the ground.

"We will keep searching, sire!" the other chipped in.

Rylan's lips pressed together in disdain. Alice had planned this out carefully, making sure to cover her tracks well. Locating her would be no easy feat. But they mustn't give up.

With hands clenched into fists, he replied, "See that you do."

"Yes, Your Majesty!" they shouted in chorus with another bow before racing off in the opposite direction. He stared after them for a few moments, his dread taking a deeper root within him and climbing up every limb in his body.

If he didn't find Alice soon and gain back his heart, Wonderland could be doomed to earth-shattering destruction.

SHE DOZES IN BLACK ROSES

What kind of addresses are these? Ellie thought to herself the moment she unrolled the parchment and glanced over its words. For a moment, she thought King Rhapsody had given her the wrong list, but there at the end, he left a note specifically telling her to successfully complete the first task given to her as the new gardener.

But every word she read seemed to whack a stick at her intelligence until she finally understood why the people here seemed to go mad.

Two past lollipop lane.

Eighteen down the rabbit hole.

A giant's throw from the comet.

A skip and a wish at four.

Just past the caterpillar. You can't miss it.

Look for the tenth turtle under the stone.

Ellie glanced up, eyes searching for Rylan in an attempt to catch him and make him clarify his instructions, but it was as if he'd disappeared in a flash, the dark silhouette of his attire no longer visible in the light of late morning.

Or was it early afternoon?

She glanced toward the skies and frowned. Although she felt as if she'd been working for hours already, maybe even days, the sun had not moved a single inch. Or had it? Either she was delirious, or days lasted longer in the Mad Lands.

A shiver ran through her body at the thought. She needed to escape this place as soon as possible, but it would likely be an impossible feat without her magic.

No…she must find a way to restore her power first, which meant evicting this awful sigil from her wrist. If she could be bound in the first place, then she could be unbound. And when her magic finally returned, she would rain down misery on King Melgen of the likes he'd never seen before. He and his daughters will only wish for mercy.

Angrily, she plucked a pair of clippers from the belt around her waist and stooped down. She had absolutely no idea where to cut the roses or how, so she simply clipped and clipped and clipped, each stem uneven with several black petals falling to the ground at her feet.

To the wastelands with Rylan's ridiculously specific instructions! Only twelve roses at a time? What kind of foolish notion was that? And what was he going to do? Count each flower? Number every petal? Inspect her handiwork with a ruler?

Quite frankly, the roses were the least of her problems. But she would bide her time, staying out of trouble just long enough to unravel her current conundrum.

She located a half dozen vases in the greenhouse and placed them on the ground at the base of the bushes. Next, she reached for the roses she just cut to place them inside. But then she screeched in surprise when one of the vases popped out a pair of glass legs and darted away from her before coming to a standstill several arm lengths away.

"I don't have time for this!" she groaned, planting her hands on her hips and huffing at the skies. Just the thought of chasing around a living vase filled her with exhaustion. She had better things to do.

Releasing an exasperated huff, she swooped down and tried to snatch the vase for a second time, but it leaped out of the way and settled itself on a stone bench with a taunting clatter.

"Fine!" she shouted, ignoring the offending thing and reaching for a different vase altogether.

But that one, too, dodged her grab attempt and sprinted awkwardly on glass legs around a hedge and disappeared into the bushes. As if emboldened by the others, the remaining four vases squeaked excitedly and darted in different directions. She attempted to pounce on one of them, but instead of a handful of vase, she instead received a faceful of grass and sod.

The vases snickered at her, the little voices echoing from different parts of the garden as if taunting her.

One of the things peeked around a bush, squeaking again as if laughing at her. She'd had enough of people laughing at her. This time, she would be the one laughing.

She pushed herself to her feet and sprinted after a small group of vases huddled together. They scattered like a flock of chickens hunted by a fox. She chased them around bushes and hedges and then around a fountain spurting amber tea instead of water.

Lunging again, she managed to grab hold of one of the vases around the neck of the structure. It squeaked and screamed, flailing its glass legs. This time as she made her way back to the roses, holding on tight to the vase, the remaining five formed a line like ducklings waddling after their mother. When they reached her previous spot, the vases tucked their legs in and remained dutifully still.

"Now don't move," she warned, waving her clippers in front of the lot of them. "Or I *will* use this. It's good for smashing glass, too."

One of them quivered but otherwise continued to remain still.

Ellie watched them out of the corner of her eye as she cut rose after rose, placing them in six different piles and counting twelve for each pile. She swiped a hand across her forehead, the sun beating down on her and making her feel drowsy. Had the position of the sun moved? It seemed as if it now lay farther east in the sky than in the west.

Unless the directions were opposite in the Mad Lands?

She scrubbed a hand over her face, her eyes feeling heavy. Just this last task, and then she could take a break.

Mindful of the thorns on each rose, she carefully tucked the first dozen into the unruliest of the six vases. When she started on the second batch, her limbs became like lead, pulling her weight downward. She found it difficult to keep her body upright and her hands working on her task.

Heavy blinks clouded her vision for a few moments before she released a long yawn. But still, she forced herself to finish the second vase until silky petals unfurled in an ebony array of darkness. Never had she seen such a deep, rich color on a flower before. They were beautiful...

She leaned closer and inhaled the surprisingly sweet fragrance. The scent was unique, like nothing she had ever encountered. Like stardust and midnight shadow.

When her body felt even heavier than before, she leaned on one elbow and admired the beauty of the flowers, releasing yet another yawn, this one longer than the last. She blinked slowly, her mind in a daze.

Something wriggled in the back of her mind. Something the king had said earlier. But no matter how hard she pulled at the memory, it refused to budge.

She dropped from her elbow to her shoulder until she lay on the ground on her side. Her outfit was going to get dirty again if she remained on the grass for too long. But perhaps a few minutes couldn't hurt.

Unable to hold up her heavy head, she rested entirely on her side next to the vases and rose piles, her blinking slowing even more until her eyes closed entirely.

Just a little rest.

And then she would get back to work.

Just…a little…rest…

Rylan immediately knew something was wrong the moment a powerful rush of energy entered his body, a stark contrast to the steady pulses of strength he received by the hour from previous recipients of now-withering black roses.

It was as if his legs reacted on their own as he leaped up from his desk, threw open the doors to his study, and sprinted down the hallway as fast as his body had ever moved before. He didn't know why he sprang into action so quickly. His haste made little sense in the grand scheme of things. But still, that small bit of panic consumed him as raw energy, or perhaps it was from the siphoned energy slamming into his body in gigantic waves.

Someone was going to die. This was not good. He could not possibly survive such guilt again.

At first, he ran to the front steps of the castle but paused at the top of the staircase when logic barely managed to tap on his brain. He let it inside the door.

The siphoned energy couldn't have come from his previous targets, as most of the magic had likely been eaten up by now. If the new gardener had done her job correctly, then six recipients would have received exactly a dozen roses each. Just enough to absorb energy but not enough for it to be overly noticeable.

To absorb *this* much energy, however...

"Flapping goose wings!" he muttered under his breath as he leaped over the railing in a single bound and landed deftly on his feet in soft grass. If anyone saw the display, no one commented, and certainly nobody stopped him.

He wasn't sure what possessed him to rush to this person's aid. He knew he shouldn't care about a sorceress. But something in him screamed at him to keep this person alive. He rushed into the garden gates situated between two rows of hedges, and from there, a powerfully sweet fragrance filled his nose, confirming his suspicions and inspiring alarm to flicker on and off within his chest.

Energy continued to slam into him, but it was almost too much. Because on the other end, it was taking a life he had not meant to take.

His breaths came in rasps as he stumbled into the rose garden, past blooms of pink, gold, and blue, and into the farthest corner hidden away from the rest of the flowers.

A heady sweetness filled the air, sticky with mischief and destruction. For a moment, he stood frozen as each breath filled him with strength and vigor. He wanted more. For every fiber of his limbs to grow stronger, for his body to no longer know weakness.

But then he blinked several times, breaking himself out of his own crafty spell. He spun in a circle, frantically glancing around. Until he spotted her.

Ellie lay sprawled on the ground, her auburn curls hiding most of her face in her fetal position. Dozens of black roses—*cut* black roses—lay scattered around her, as only one of the vases were filled. She hadn't even managed to fill the second vase before the roses' fragrance had claimed her.

"Why didn't you listen to me?" he gasped, but his words fell on deaf, unconscious ears.

He watched her intently, searching for the rise and fall of every breath. But he didn't find it.

And there, he ran into a conundrum.

He glanced down at his gloved hands as indecision warred within him. Years had passed since he'd touched another person, and he dared not try again. But…

But…

Desperation clung to him like the annoying barbs of a wabbernabber as he glanced up, searching for someone else within the vicinity to help him. However, no such person existed. He was alone. And this woman was dying.

The window to act grew smaller by the second. But he still felt her energy becoming his. She was still alive.

Panic continued to grow larger inside him. He clutched either side of his head and turned in a slow circle. *Not again not again not again.* He couldn't do this again.

But he must.

He needed a gardener. He couldn't afford her getting sick or dying. Not now of all times. And especially not from his roses.

Yes, that was it. Nothing more. Nothing less.

And so, with a deep, steadying breath, Rylan Rhapsody stooped down and scooped the woman into his arms, touching someone for the very first time in a very long time.

6
Painting The Roses Red

A strange warmth filled Rylan's chest, right where his heart should be. The temperature rose within him, a peculiar feeling when he had otherwise felt cold and aloof ever since losing the Heart of Wonderland.

The woman in his arms lay limp against him, but she didn't start convulsing at his touch, nor did she gasp with breath as if something heavy crushed her lungs. Rather, her previously pale face gained a little more color. Not much. But a little.

Curiosity flared within him, momentarily pushing out the intense fear that usually clung to the inner walls of his now-non-existent heart. He adjusted his grip on her and slowly lifted his hand, his gloved finger inching toward her face. Could he? *Should* he?

But before his hand made contact with her cheek, another burst of power and energy surged into him. He almost dropped her in alarm. Until he realized he still stood next to the black roses as they continued to release their sweet, heady aroma.

He hurried away from the roses with long strides, holding gingerly onto her while trying his utmost not to touch her with his hands, even gloved. It made for a silly sight with his fingers splayed out in his effort not to make contact with her as much as possible.

Ellie's face had lost the color it had previously gained, and for a moment, panic once more threatened for his arms to drop her. However, he quickly realized her loss of consciousness and energy had been from the roses. They no longer siphoned her lifeforce from her when separated from the flowers.

Frustration dug its claws into his anxious mind when no servants appeared as he entered the castle. He didn't want to hold this woman. *Not again. Not again. Not again.* But he found little choice in the matter when the only other option was to abandon her on the spotless white carpets underfoot.

Why do I care? he silently asked himself, gritting his teeth until his jaw ached. He continued to move quickly through the hallways with his hands and fingers stiff to keep from touching her. *She's a sorceress. A witch.*

Shaking his head in confusion, he climbed to the guest wing of the castle, kicked open one of the doors with his foot, and shuffled awkwardly inside as he tried to keep from hitting the woman's head against the doorframe.

He dropped her onto the bed in a heap, forgetting to be gentle when handling her. He didn't really know *how* to be gentle. It's been so long since he'd handled anyone at all.

Placing his hands on his hips, he stared at her with brows furrowed. "Well. Anyways…"

Now what?

What did one do with an ailing person? Especially one from the upper world?

"Ah! I have it." He hastily picked up the water basin against the wall, frowning when he found blue flower petals floating aimlessly on top. Right! He forgot he'd asked the last gardener to surreptitiously scatter them about the room to use against a visiting dignitary. Well, it was too late now. Besides, the petals were likely too diluted to tell the future anyway.

Without another thought, he dumped the water over the sorceress's head and waited. No gasp of shock. No bolting upright. She remained still.

He grabbed a cold fire poker by the hearth, turned it around in his hands, and poked her shoulder with the blunt end of it.

Nothing.

Was she…dead?

He was just about to prod her again when images slammed into his mind, startling him and completely taking him by surprise. He stumbled backward, grasping for anything within reach but only managed to slam his hand against the edge of a second basin, tripping to the ground just as the water splashed over his own head.

And then his surroundings disappeared entirely, replaced by brief, flashing images. A mushroom forest. A raging river. The silhouette of a worn shack. An eerie room. But then the images halted, focusing on a bright red object pulsing with a crimson light.

It was no ordinary crystal.

The way it pulsed and pounded, shimmering with otherworldly light…

The Heart of Wonderland.

In a moment of panicked hope, Rylan attempted to reach out for his heart, but his fingers touched air rather than something tangible. He tried again only to face the same results. This was the future. A vision. He could not interact with it, only observe.

But then shock jolted up his throat when the color green formed at the edge of his vision. Fabric. Clothing. It was a dress. And then the person wearing it came more into focus, wearing a purple cloak over the green gown, but the hood obscured her face.

She stood behind the pedestal with her hands hovering over the heart, not quite touching. The woman stared transfixed at the glowing crystal, and a sense of possessiveness overcame him.

He wanted to scream, "*Halt, that's mine! Hands off!*"

But words refused to form on his tongue as if he found himself in a dream-like state with no true will of his own. He wanted to smack her hands. Push her backward. Grab his heart and run. However, his body remained frozen.

A door slammed on the opposite end of the room, and the woman jerked her head upward to find the source of the noise.

Only then did the shadows lift from her face enough for him to view what lay beneath.

Shock once again hit him at full force, and he couldn't help but stare in bewildered disbelief. He knew that face. It belonged to…

Ellie Strife.

The vision lurched in a disorienting manner, and he threw his head back to catch himself, only to hiss between his teeth when his head smacked against something hard.

He found himself back in his palace, sprawled on the ground with his back to a cabinet. Water dripped from his black hair and onto his clothing, a chill shooting through him that had nothing to do with the spilled basin.

The sorceress!

He scrambled to his feet and strode toward the bed, all while his head pounded something fierce. He never enjoyed using the blue roses, as they were disorienting and painful for his mind. Not to mention accidentally hurting himself in the process.

He stared down at the sleeping woman in a new, hopeful light. If she had been in the vision of the future, then she was capable of locating the Heart of Wonderland. She could help him find its whereabouts…

Someone like her would never help him, and he refused to admit he needed that help. But if she were to do it willingly against her will?

His mouth lifted in a half-grin as he thought of his roses. Particularly, his *red* roses. The easiest way to get someone to do what he wanted? Make them fall in love with him.

This witch he had spared from the ax had suddenly become of great interest to him. Now it would only be a matter of time before he found exactly what he wanted.

A rumbling sensation startled Ellie awake. Her hand shot out to brace herself against a soft bedspread while the other lifted to protect her head. But nothing fell on top of her. Rather, the earth beneath her quaked, rattling the windows and picture frames on the walls.

After several moments, the tremors ceased, and once again all was still.

She shot upright, her eyes opening wide when she found herself in an unfamiliar room with a foreign white ceiling with gold trim above her. For a moment, her disoriented mind tried to recall where she was and why. But her question was soon answered when she felt a dangerous presence in the room with her.

Dangerous and wily and entirely unpredictable.

Her gaze darted toward one of the windows. King Rylan Rhapsody perched delicately on the sill with ankles crossed, his black cloak draped elegantly over one shoulder. He brought a red rose to his nose and inhaled its scent before twirling the stem between gloved fingers.

Her stare fixed onto the rose and refused to let go. Especially now that she realized what they were. She was not ignorant, as she had been a sorceress likely twenty times longer than the king had been alive. She recognized magic when she encountered it, and those roses were full of it.

She berated herself for not recognizing her first encounter with the white rose upon meeting the king, but after the black roses… The way they had stolen the energy from her body… There was no mistaking it.

But should she feign ignorance? If Rylan was so powerful as to nearly kill her with a few dozen roses alone, what could he do when he actually tried to harm her?

A wild and unpredictable man was one of the most dangerous of them all.

In the end, she decided to play ignorant. A sorceress never revealed her hand until it benefitted her the most.

"What happened?" she croaked. At least she didn't have to fake her dry throat. "Where am I?"

Slowly, the king approached her bedside and handed her a glass of water. She took it hesitantly, worried that some sort of rose extract might be hiding inside. But as she pressed the rim of the glass to her lips, she furtively inhaled to search for any trace of a strange aroma. She found none.

Therefore, she allowed herself a few sips.

His demeanor remained relaxed and uncaring as he turned a chair around and sat on it backwards. "You exhausted yourself and fell asleep while attending to your duties."

"And I ended up here? How?"

"I found you in the garden a few hours ago."

The water went down wrong, and she coughed and coughed until she managed to gain better control of herself. Her gaze darted toward the window where sunlight shone through the glass.

"But...but it's still light outside."

Unexpectedly, he burst into laughter, his golden eyes sparkling. "You've been at the palace for days! Don't you know how Wonderland works?" He dug into his pocket and pulled out a pocket watch. "It's currently eighteen after the croaking frog."

She stared at him incredulously, trying to wrap her mind around his words. She'd been here for days? But...but... She hadn't slept in all that time because she'd thought the day just felt abnormally long! No wonder she'd been downright exhausted.

"What does that even mean?" she cried exasperatedly.

Laughing again, he tapped on the glass of his watch. The hand spun several times, the numbers switching around, until coming to a standstill. "Every thirty minutes is a new marker. In twelve minutes, it will be screaming shrills on the dot."

Again, she blinked at him, hardly believing her ears. Was she starting to go batty as well? Was that what this was?

His grin only widened as he pointed to the sky outside the window. "Thirty minutes until midnight," he clarified for her. "And don't look at me like that. I'm not entirely unaware of the workings of the upper world."

"But…but it's light outside." Yep, she was losing it in the head.

"Yes, well, our light doesn't rise in the east and set in the west." He laughed again, his eyes sparkling with mischief. "We never know if our days are going to be light or dark, so most of us carry time on our person."

The more Ellie learned about the Mad Lands, the less she realized she understood. Nothing made sense here. Nothing at all! This place didn't follow the logical patterns of the world she knew.

"But why?" A hint of desperation clung to her voice, begging him to make this place make sense.

However, he only gestured to the window with a tilt of his head. Her eyebrows furrowed in confusion but then widened in alarm. She tried to jump to her feet, but fatigue dragged her back to the bed, forcing her to watch the window helplessly.

The ground shook and shuddered like the beat of a steady drum, an entirely different rhythm of tremors from the one before. An enormous giant as tall as the willowing clouds raced along the hills, looking as if its mighty footfalls might crush everything beneath its feet without caring whether it was alive.

"Your Highness!" she cried out in warning, but the king simply stood there watching as if he were gazing at a calm sea rather than a rampaging giant.

The giant raised a large hand and swatted the sun. Actually swatted! The sun leaped across the sky with the force of the blow until it disappeared beneath the distant hills. A sudden darkness fell upon the land, and only then did glittering moonlight rain down from the heavens. But *actual* glitter. Almost like snow. But it disappeared before touching the ground.

Outside the window, the giant's shrill laughter slammed into the foundation of the castle before it chased after the sun it had just smacked away.

Ellie shook her head in bewilderment. What...what...?

Rylan gasped, his hand flying to his chest. "Would you look at that! I have not seen the moon in weeks. What a beautiful sight."

"Weeks?!"

He nonchalantly waved a hand. "Details, darling. Details. Besides, now the forest will glow, and I'm very much looking forward to it."

Once again, her gaze darted toward the hills where the giant had disappeared. "Is that the source of the tremors?" she asked.

Rylan paused for a moment before answering. "...No."

"Then what is?"

He shrugged and turned a shoulder to her. "Who knows?"

The way he positioned himself away from her made her suspicious that he might be hiding something.

She commented, "Just one of his feet could have squashed the palace."

"He wouldn't."

"Why?"

Another wave of his fingers. "Oh, he likes anything golden. I once gifted him a goose that laid golden eggs. Now he leaves Wonderland alone with all his fumbling and stumbling." He laughed, his eyes lighting up. "Fumbling. Stumbling. Humbling. Jumbling. Bumbling. Crumbling. Grumbling. Mumb—"

"What are you doing?" she gasped, staring at him as if he were a wild dog that might snap at her out of unpredictability alone. Just when she thought he might not actually be mad, he blindfolded her senses and spun her around a few hundred times until she didn't know what was up and what was down.

"Rhyming, of course! A good exercise for the mind."

Her heart raced uncomfortably at the thought. How much time must someone spend in the Mad Lands until they turn mad? She needed to leave this place. As soon as possible. Lest she meet the same fate as the king.

But before that, she needed answers.

"Did you…you know…" She dragged a hand across her throat. "The last gardener?"

He gave her an appalling look. "Who do you think I am? Of course, I did!" Just when some of the color drained from her face, he gave her a half grin. "All jests. I sent him to work in the caterpillar fields." He shuddered. "That place gives me the jitters."

She grimaced. "I hope I never find out what that is."

"Ha! Well, at this rate, you're well on your way."

The king's expression transitioned from levity to seriousness in the space of a moment, inspiring a sense of dread in the deepest pit of her stomach. She sensed magic in the air. But what kind? And where?

However, when he lifted the red rose to his nose once again, she understood.

"I'm glad you are recovering," he said, all mirth gone from his eyes. "This is for you."

He held out the rose to her. Instinct may have once told her to take the gift from him, but after the incident with the black roses… She didn't dare.

"I-I-I think you've got the wrong i-i-impression about us," she stuttered instead, cursing herself as she did so.

His mouth lifted in a half smirk. "And what impression might that be?"

Still, he held out the rose, waiting for her to accept it.

Swallowing the strange anxiety building up in her throat, she clutched onto the soft bed sheets to keep herself from reaching out. "I am perfectly aware of the meaning of a red rose."

"Which is what?" he asked innocently, and perhaps the question might have been innocent if not for his smirk growing wider with the perfect curve of his mouth.

"I-I-I need to get back to work." She wasn't sure why her chest squeezed within her, nor why her pulse thrummed at her neck like the quiet whisper of a butterfly's wings. She only knew she needed to escape the jaws of the lion already holding her within its grasp. Teasing her. Playing with her. Waiting for her to bolt before he pounced.

But like the prey, she couldn't help but bolt.

The moment she put weight on her legs, she realized she underestimated exactly how much strength she currently possessed in her body. Within two steps, she collapsed to the lush carpet with a shriek, taking raspy breaths while on her hands and knees.

Rylan rushed to her side and reached for her as if to help her up, but at the last moment, he retracted his hands and took several steps backward as if she carried a disease. Perhaps the lion was no longer fond of playing with his food.

With an air of nonchalance, he turned away from her and tucked the red rose into a vase—one that didn't run away, the vexing pests—the petals glistening crimson like large droplets of blood. "The red ones smell the sweetest. I hope you enjoy them as much as I do."

She trailed him with her gaze as he left the room, closing the door behind him with a soft click. After a few moments of silence, she warily eyed the red solitary rose in the vase beside the bed, her thoughts whirring quickly in her mind.

She knew the white ones forced the truth out of someone. Unfortunately, she now understood the power of the black roses after they'd stolen her energy and life force. But what about red?

Determination stole across her features as she shakily climbed to her feet. The risk of trying to fool a sorceress was getting caught in your own web. And now? Rylan's hands were covered in sticky threads. One wrong touch, and the entire structure would unravel.

Ellie's mouth lifted in a smirk.

Now…where was the paint?

7
Mad Time at Tea o'Clock

Making someone fall in love is such a hassle, Rylan thought to himself as he drummed his fingers against the wooden table filled to the brim with tea, sweet confections, porcelain, and everything in between.

Not only hadn't he felt the stirrings of one-sided love through his magic roses, but Ellie was not trailing him around like a lovesick whopperknopper like she ought to. Either she hadn't pricked herself on the rose, or she was immune to his charms.

He waved the ridiculous notion away with his hand. No one was immune to his charms.

Glancing toward the skies, he noted the shimmers of moonlight fluttering overhead, most of it blocked by the boughs of trees surrounding the clearing. At tea o'clock, the absence of the sun was disorienting, even in Wonderland. A part of him wondered what Ellie's world looked like. A predictable sun. Time that ebbed and flowed with its movements. And *snow*. He'd never seen snow. One day, perhaps he could.

"Your Highness," a female voice said behind him. "You asked to see me?"

Rylan forked a piece of rackleberry tart into his mouth and ignored the gardener. He'd speak to her when he felt like it.

But then she said, "Your shoe is on the wrong foot."

He couldn't stop his gaze from darting downward, only to scowl when he found his shoes on the correct feet. He turned his scowl toward her and the smirk playing on the corners of her mouth. This certainly was a person who didn't tolerate being ignored.

Changing his tune, he stood up and smiled, and each of his friends stood as well following his example. "Ah! Ellie Strife. Welcome to our tea party. You're right on time. Why don't you take a seat?"

He pulled out a chair next to himself, and her previous smirk immediately fell into something a bit more wary. But once she sat, his friends pulled her into one conversation after the other, adopting her like a hen to an orphaned chick. Piper Pixiewing, especially, latched onto Ellie's chair and pulled it closer, whispering something into her ear. Both women snickered and glanced his way, Piper's wings casting a rainbow of light across the table with a flutter of wind.

Rylan tried his best not to scowl. He hadn't brought Ellie here to win over his friends. He'd brought her because she had something he wanted. He'd do anything to get his heart back, including using her.

"Try this!" Gideon Glimmer said as he pushed a towering plate of plum-paste buns in front of her. "It tastes like a breath of spring in full blossom."

Only after a moment of hesitation, Ellie picked up one of the buns. Despite himself, he couldn't help but tease.

"If you eat any food in Wonderland, you're bound here for the rest of your life."

Her hand paused mid-air, the bun halfway to her mouth.

"He's jesting!" Gideon said, clapping her on the shoulder. "Our King of Hearts enjoys teasing far too much."

Rylan held up a placating hand. "It's true. I do." And then he reached toward the middle of the table and plucked a single crimson rose from a crystal vase. The vase squawked before clambering off the table and running in the direction of the castle.

Suddenly, his entire group of friends diverted their attention elsewhere, busy conversing with one another rather than paying attention to him and Ellie. He felt their attention on them all the same.

He inhaled the scent of the rose, his nose wrinkling the slightest bit when the smell was off. It was probably because the food's aroma contributed to the dulling of his senses.

"Please accept this," he murmured quietly, trying to sound as sincere as possible as he offered the rose to her, "as a token of friendship."

Unlike the last time, she accepted the rose and inhaled its fragrance as well. However, she quickly hissed between her teeth and retracted her hand, revealing the single droplet of blood on her finger.

This is it! He barely restrained his excitement. His heart was just within reach. Now he needed a little bit of shamelessness, and he'd have her within his pocket.

"You look deep in thought." He grinned, resting his chin in his hand. "Thinking good thoughts about me, perhaps?"

Something sparked in her eyes, and he barely restrained a grin wanting to escape past a smug expression.

"Oh, I'm having thoughts, absolutely."

She leaned closer to him, her long eyelashes casting dark shadows across the deep brown of her irises as she gazed at him with the moon reflecting in her eyes.

It worked! he gloated internally. His roses never ceased giving.

"Don't you want to ask what those thoughts are?" Her fingers walked across the table toward him, stopping right before his sleeve. Close but not touching.

His smugness grew to new heights at her boldness. "And what are those thoughts?"

All too suddenly, her eyebrows furrowed together as she pointed aggressively toward his chest, again not touching. "I thought you were a scoundrel, but this proves it. Trying to make me fall in love with you? How brazen can you be? The nerve!"

His eyes flashed wide open in shock, his attention darting to the rose she held in her hands when the wrongness of the situation clicked in his mind. It was no wonder it smelled differently than usual. The red rose was not actually a red rose.

It was white.

And judging by the grin on the woman's lips, she was aware of it, too.

He laughed out loud, drawing far too much attention from his friends. But he couldn't help himself. The King of Hearts had been outplayed.

Crossing his arms, he shook his head at her, not bothering to deny anything at this point. Cajoling and tricking were not going to work on this one. But still, he moved away from the table, and she followed him until they were barely out of earshot of the others.

Ellie smirked at him. The audacity! Never had he been caught in a trap so thoroughly set by a sorceress, especially without her magic. He'd been arrogant. Overly confident. She'd played him right into her trap, and he hadn't even seen it coming.

"Now..." she murmured, batting her eyelashes at him. "You will tell me exactly how to break my curse. Otherwise..." Slowly, she tipped her head toward his friends, who continued chattering around the table. However, he felt some of their stares on him and Ellie. Lowering her voice, she finished with, "Otherwise, I will tell them what your roses do. What will happen then?"

"Stop," he warned.

But she didn't heed him as she walked in a slow circle around him like a predator sizing up their prey. "How many of your friends and subjects have you used? How many have you controlled or manipulated through your power?" She tsked as she came to stand in front of him once more. "How many friends would you have left once I plant the seed of doubt in their minds?"

Rylan clenched his jaw and fists simultaneously. He'd always been careful with his roses. A little here. A little there. Nearly imperceptible. Never enough to draw notice. Careful and calculated. But never on his friends. However, if they found out what he could really do?

Of course, he'd always told himself it was necessary. That he'd had no choice. But for her to expose him to some of the only people he cared about?

He crossed his arms and feigned nonchalance, regretting not sending her to lose her mind in the Cheshire's presence after all. "You want to learn how to break your curse?" He sneered at her and tipped his head to the side. "It's easy. You're overthinking the solution. But I'm not much in a giving mood today, so..."

He lifted his hands and inspected his nails, though all for show because he still wore gloves over his fingers.

"Does the threat of revealing your secrets not suffice?" Her teeth clamped together with a click like a lioness biting down on air instead of her prey. "What do you want? I may be willing to trade."

Her attention bore into him as he casually tapped a finger against his chin as if lost in thought. "There is something I want." He leveled her with a stare, and unexpectedly, his stomach clenched when met by the ferociousness of her gaze. Intense. Unyielding.

"Name it. Though, I may not be in such a giving mood either."

Despite his best efforts to hold himself back, his lips curled up at the corners. Such fire. Such passion and burning *hatred*. But who was the hatred pointed toward? Himself? Or something else entirely?

Rylan stepped backward to place a little more distance between himself and the tea party. The sorceress followed with a step forward. "There is a little trinket I want to find. Nothing too important." Ha! As if the Heart of Wonderland was a mere doodad. "If you help me find this, I will tell you how to break your curse."

"Assuming you even know how. You might be lying."

He held up his hand and lowered his gaze. "Upon my very soul, I swear no lies that I pull."

"Did you just rhyme again?"

"No," he scoffed. "Perhaps you ought to check your hearing. Do you want to make this deal or not?"

"Fine." She held out a hand, but he only stared at her with a disgruntled expression. He refused to touch her. Never again. "But if I discover any trickery, you will know the wrath of a sorceress."

He coughed into his hand and murmured, "You have to have magic to make threats like that." He coughed again and peeked at her with a mischievous grin.

She glared.

Oh, how he enjoyed making her mad! What fun.

Rather than shaking her hand to seal the deal, he lifted his own instead to swear an oath. "I swear to you that once we find this trinket, I will tell you all you need to know. No trickery. No lies. I will be on my best behavior."

Although suspicion still lingered in her eyes, she appeared to contemplate his deal. "Your best behavior changes based on the time of day."

"You wound me!" He placed his hand over his face as if upset over her words, but he still peeked at her between his fingers.

Finally, she sighed. "Deal. When do we set out?"

"This very moment," he replied with a spring in his step, bidding farewell to his friends before setting out on a path through the woods in the darkness of the Wonderland afternoon.

"I'm not ready to go."

"You should have thought about that before attending a tea party, no? Let's depart!"

Her steps paused, but then she sighed and followed behind. Now, it was only a matter of time before he was reunited with his heart. Hopefully before any more of his roses died, and his soul withered along with them.

8
QUEEN OF SPADES

"Soooo," Ellie started, glancing at the Mad King from the corner of her eye as they walked along a quiet, serene path through the woods. "This trinket. What exactly is it?"

Her attention didn't remain on him for long. It was impossible when the magical and mystical surrounded her in the form of glowing blue mushrooms and sparkling moon beams glistening from the skies. The upper world had nothing like this. Beautiful. Enchanting. Entirely otherworldly.

The strangest sensation of safety enveloped her in Rylan's presence. When she first arrived in Wonderland, she'd raced through these very woods with terror ripping through her soul. But now? She wondered what she'd been afraid of in the first place. It was almost as if the king's presence alone chased away all the nefarious creatures meaning her harm.

Rylan flipped his hand through the air in a nonchalant manner. "Like I said, it's nothing too important. Something a former friend stole from me. But I'd like it back all the same."

Despite his words, Ellie sensed tension strung tight within his speech. He wanted it more than he was letting on.

"How do you know where to find it?" she asked as they passed by a glowing mushroom five times her size, but low enough to barely pass over her head. Her curiosity got the best of her, and she lifted her hand to trail her fingers over the spongy underbottom of the fungus. She sensed nothing magical within the textured membrane. It was just an ordinary mushroom. But large. And glowy.

"I just do."

"And you need my help...why?"

They ducked beneath a hanging vine and climbed over a low, squishy mushroom blocking their path.

Rylan laughed, his eyes sparkling with mischief. "As cannon fodder, of course. Why else?"

She scowled when she couldn't tell if he was serious. There must have been a reason—a real reason—for him to request her presence over other more qualified candidates. He'd even left his guards behind at the palace. There must have been a good explanation for it.

Unless...

Unless he was serious.

A shudder ran down her spine at the thought. She'd prefer not becoming cannon fodder for whatever unknown reason.

Therefore, she needed to remain useful in a place so foreign and confusing. Survival was at the top of her to-do list.

Suddenly, Ellie's eyes widened, and she leaped backward on the defensive while pointing to an orange-pink ball of fur the size of her fist sitting in the middle of the road by its lonesome.

"Watch out!" she screeched. "It's one of those…those…creatures!"

"A kneazle?" He raised his eyebrow at her, a look of confusion on his face. His lips twitched, but then his eyes widened with horror to mirror her own. "We'd better run! Go, go, go!"

She didn't need to be told twice. She turned on her heel, her boots scrambling for purchase on the slippery mushroom terrain. She stepped on her skirt amid her stumbling but quickly caught her balance and increased her pace.

To her horror, the kneazle had transformed into a creature the size of her head, sharp teeth gleaming beneath the forest mushroom glow, as it hopped after them with murder in its hypnotizing eyes.

"Faster!" she screeched. "Faster! It's catching up to us."

They took twists and turns within the forest, venturing deeper into the trees to try to escape their pursuer. But no matter where they went, the creature followed.

They'd get eaten for sure! She had been lucky last time. Surely, her luck had long since run out.

Her lungs burned with the strain of flight. When her legs ached and each breath felt like agony, she wanted nothing more to escape to a place of safety. But where? Could those creatures climb trees?

She recalled the way the kneazles had traveled in a group and shuddered. If they trapped themselves within the boughs of a tree, what waited for them at the bottom would soon be rather unpleasant.

Therefore, they kept running.

They were both painfully out of air and gasping for each breath. They rounded the corner, only to skid to a complete stop when they found the kneazle waiting in the middle of the road with burning red eyes and sharp fangs protruding from its mouth.

Rylan stepped in front of her and placed his hand on the hilt of his sword. "Don't worry, darling. I'll attack it with my..." His words trailed off as he pulled his weapon from its scabbard. "...flower."

Instead of a sword scraping from the scabbard, a wilted flower the entire length of his arm now hung limp in Rylan's hand.

"Huh..." he murmured. "That's new."

"What do you mean?" she cried. "Where's your sword?"

He shrugged. "Such an angry tone. It's not my fault my weapon decided to be lazy today!"

"For the love of everything magical!" Ellie shouted, throwing her hands in the air while contemplating whether to kick a tree in her frustration. But surely with her luck, the effort would only break her leg or knock something terrifying from the boughs overhead. "Can't anything in these blasted Mad Lands go right?"

"Sure, they can," he said with a charming grin. "You just have to learn to adapt."

He lunged forward and tapped the small beast on the top of the head with the flower. Pollen burst out of its spores and created a plume of dust. The creature sneezed and sat back on its haunches, momentarily stunned by confusion. Its fangs disappeared as it turned back into a ball of fluff, its eyes wide and innocent, the monster hidden deep within its outer appearance.

All too suddenly, Rylan dropped the flower weapon and cupped his face in his hands, gazing at the creature with sparkles in his eyes. "Dawwww. It's so cute!"

"Not cute. Not cute!" She stooped down to grab the flower weapon and held it in both her hands while pointing it toward the malicious thing.

Despite her words, Rylan approached the creature and picked it up, cupped it in both his hands, and nuzzled his cheek against its light orange fur. "How can you resist such a face? I think I'm going to keep it."

"You cannot keep the demon kneazle!" For a man who didn't touch anyone, he certainly seemed to have no qualms about picking up dangerous critters.

He ignored her and nuzzled it again until it emitted a soft purr. Both the creature and the man gave her a manipulative pouty smile. "We'll name him Peachy Puff."

"No, no, no! Those things chased me out of the forest with sharp teeth by the bucketfuls."

Rylan gestured to her with a sweep of her hand. "Your only mistake was running. They like to give chase."

For a moment, she stared at him with wide, stupefied eyes as her mind spun in circles, trying to make sense of *anything* the Mad King said or did. "So… This entire time that we've been running…"

He grinned, but she sensed teasing maliciousness behind the action. "A game. I enjoyed it immensely. Didn't you?"

Her jaw dropped as she stared back at him incredulously. They'd been running for what felt like hours. Her screams… Her fear… Her belief that the creature would catch up to them with its friends and tear them apart piece by piece with sharp, unyielding teeth? And this was only a game to him?

A scowl darkened her expression, and he at least had the decency to run when she chased after him with the weapon. He ducked behind a tree just as she struck out with the pollen-inducing flower and hit the trunk rather than him. A plume of powder escaped with the attack.

"Oh, if I had my magic, I'd turn you into a toad! A toad, Your Madness!" She attacked again, only for him to duck away, and she smacked the tree again with his flower sword. "And you'd be forced to croak every night and sleep under lily pads." Another smack. "And no one would want to break your curse. Because you are ridiculous!" Smack. "And terrible!" Smack. "And you deserve." Smack. "To be." Smack. "A toad!"

On the last smack, the weapon transformed from a flower to a sword, slicing across the trunk with its sharp edge.

Rylan perked up and rounded the tree, snatching the weapon from her grasp and inspecting its blade. "Ah! Back to normal. Many thanks, kind lady."

"Ugh!" she shouted, throwing her hands up and stomping away in the opposite direction as him. She didn't care where she was going as long as it was somewhere he wasn't.

"I wouldn't go that way!" he called after her.

She ignored him. What did he know? He was likely only teasing her again.

When he didn't follow, she glanced over her shoulder to find him leaning against the trunk of a tree while cooing to his new little pet, telling it how much of a good boy it was while complementing the color of its sunset fur. He didn't try to stop her again, but he clearly wasn't going to trail behind her.

Her footsteps hesitated on the dirt path beneath her feet when she noticed the trampled foliage and a strong, magical aura of dread burrowed into the air. A high-pitched shriek sent birds flying out of the boughs overhead in a deafening array of twittering and frightened squawks.

The person shrieked a second time before heavy footfalls sounded in her direction. A woman appeared, her eyes bloodshot, her breaths frantic, and her expression crazed. She ran past Ellie without a second glance while covering her ears as if a terrible sound grated against her mind.

Ellie's gaze darted back down the path the woman had fled from, the dread in the air only seeming to magnify by the second. But as she turned back around to follow, the path had disappeared entirely, the woman nowhere in sight.

The air became heavier, more difficult to breathe with each passing moment. Darkness rolled in like a blanket of fog crawling across ocean waters and obscuring the path ahead.

She made the mistake of turning around again until her senses were disoriented, and her feet lost the path entirely until she had no idea which way she'd entered in the first place.

Think, Ellie, think.

Closing her eyes, she tried to focus on finding her way out of the fog. Not for the first time, she reached for her magic, only to find it blocked.

Her next idea was to call to Rylan for help, but her pride refused to bow down to the man who had warned her not to enter this area in the first place. She could get out of here. On her own.

Somewhere in the fog, a voice floated on the wind. Somewhere but nowhere at the same time. She spotted the flick of a purple tail, followed by what almost seemed to be a grin. But the images disappeared just as quickly, confusing her mind. The area rippled around her until dark shapes formed within the fog. Dark, familiar shapes.

Her breath fled from her when she recognized King Melgren, except he was younger. Just like when she'd first fallen in love. He'd promised the world to her, used her for her magic, and he'd betrayed her just as quickly.

Through the sudden ringing in her ears, she couldn't make sense of what he said. His lips moved, but the words were quickly drowned. He held out his hand to her, speaking once again. This time, a figure stopped beside him. A small, petite little thing in a dress larger than her entire frame. The woman Melgren had left Ellie for.

"No!" Ellie shouted, taking a step backward. "You lied to me! You betrayed me!"

He thrust his hand forward again, but rather than taking it, she stumbled backward until she tripped over her own shoe and landed hard on the ground.

The figures warped in front of her, growing larger with long necks, sharp teeth, and eyes gleaming with malicious intent. Their dangerous snouts snapped toward her.

Ellie screamed.

"Hold still, won't you?" Rylan grunted with the effort to keep Ellie from thrashing about on the ground by holding each arm down with the press of his boots. To touch her with his hands might kill her, but his boots? Perhaps not. But he currently found no other way to restrain her. "You're going to hurt yourself."

Sure enough, she managed to wrestle one arm free from his hold and smacked herself in the face, screaming yet again as if she saw something far more sinister than him hovering over her. She tried to smack him next, but before her hand touched his knee, he leaped backward, abandoning all effort to protect her from her own mind.

He shouldn't feel bad for her. He really shouldn't. She had done this to herself despite his warning, after all.

With a sigh, he pulled out a necklace from the confines of his vest, the pendant only as large as his pinky fingernail. But with a little coaxing, the tiny greenhouse grew large enough for him to stick his hand inside and pull out a yellow rose. After the pendant shrank back down, he pricked his finger on one of the thorns before stooping down and pricking Ellie on another thorn, drawing both of their blood.

Usually, he channeled terrifying illusions into the other person before wiping their memories of it entirely. But this time, he pushed a gentle illusion into her mind to combat the power of the Cheshire Cat. Perhaps he might not have tried otherwise, but her screaming was bound to attract something far more sinister than the Cheshire. This was for survival purposes only.

Slowly, Ellie's thrashing died down, and her screams transitioned to mild whimpers. Those whimpers became deep, steadying breaths before her eyes opened, and lucidity blinked back at him, then at the flower he held in his hand.

"Now I know what the yellow roses do," she murmured exhaustedly.

"Don't make me wipe your memories," he threatened. "I will do it."

"Oh? And which color of rose does that?"

He *hmphed* to himself and turned around, facing his back to her. She knew too much already. After their first meeting, he'd never expected her to be so smart and observant. It irked him.

"Why didn't you come sooner?" she mumbled in a disoriented manner, and he thought he detected a teasing hint in her voice, but he wasn't entirely sure.

"So you can owe me another astronomical favor, of course." He grinned, and her slow hand reached out to smack him, but he easily dodged. He counted on his fingers. "I saved you by granting you an easy sentence. Then again when you passed out in the garden. And now, when you entered the Cheshire's territory of your own free will and choice. That's three times I've saved you. Now you have no leverage on me when you owe me your life or mind three times over."

"Ughhhh," she groaned, shifting to lay on her side. "How did you get it to stop, anyway?"

"Oh, nothing too difficult." He nonchalantly waved his hand. "I just shoot it with a slingshot whenever I see it."

"That's terrible!"

Ha! Coming from the woman who would have lost her mind should she have been trapped within its illusion for even a minute longer.

"What?" he asked innocently. "I've never actually hit it. The thing disappears before I can. Besides, better to lose a stone than to lose your mind." She gave him a look that said he'd lost his marbles long ago. "At least entirely." He winked.

She mumbled something else that sounded a bit too much like an insult before her eyelids fluttered closed.

He sighed as he started a fire several paces away from where Ellie lay to help keep her warm during the night. He perched on top of a large boulder and crossed his legs beneath him, the chill seeping through his clothing. If Ellie would only listen to him rather than strike out on her own, things might just go well for her in Wonderland. But instead, she chose to run amok and take her chances.

Peachy Puff squeaked beside him, and he couldn't help but smile softly at the small creature. Animals weren't affected by his magic. Therefore, he felt confident to take off a glove and pet him with his bare hand.

However, he froze when he found something on his wrist that shouldn't be there. Something very, very, very wrong and terrifying.

He stared at his right wrist in disbelief. Emblazoned on his skin was a black spade. Prominent. Unmistakable. Claiming and grounding and a wholly unwelcome sight for his sore eyes. This could only have happened if he'd touched someone. If he'd found his match. His fated person. His other half.

And he'd only ever touched one woman in many many *many* years.

He clenched his fist as disbelief shook him to the core.

Ellie Strife, a flaring flopping flabbergasting gardener of a sorceress, was his Queen of Spades.

9

Race Against The Clock

Rylan stared down at his wrist in disbelief, the movement from the firelight flickering a shadow across the black spade symbol emblazoned on his skin. When his father had met his mother, they'd shared similar symbols on their wrists after a brief touch in a midnight ballroom. He'd heard they were inseparable after the fact.

But this…

This…

He shook his head, still unable to grasp the truth of the situation even though it bore a hole through his face with its stare. Ellie was from the upper world. A sorceress. And who even knew how old she was? She could be a thousand years old for all he knew.

Not to mention the little tidbit where he was more likely to kill her the next time he touched her than to court her properly like he may have done in another life. Besides, he wasn't interested in courtship at all. The only thing that mattered was finding his heart and solidifying his place on the Wonderland throne.

A fit of madness overtook him as his mind darkened, and his surroundings spun. He scratched and scratched at his wrist, pushing past the pain, enduring the sting as he attempted to scrub away what fate had so rudely thrust upon him. But even as his skin turned red and raw, leaving skin and blood beneath his fingernails, the spade remained.

No, no, no, no, no! He was not having this. The King of Hearts ruled alone with no other sitting beside him. Especially not *her*. Not the witch.

Not the witch!

His chest heaved with each heavy breath as he stared at his wrist, his eyes bloodshot and all warmth gone from his face. Although difficult, he attempted to reach for clarity, for reason.

Yes, Ellie might have been the only woman he'd touched in a long time, but that didn't necessarily mean she was his fated person. It must have been a fluke. Yes! Of course! Fate was teasing him. Making him see things. The spade wasn't really there. And if it was, it resided on the wrong person.

Of course, of course, of course, of course.

He mumbled to himself, "Course, source, hoarse, norse." He slapped himself on the forehead to put his mind back to rights. The mark reminded him of his mother, which reminded him of the witch long ago, which reminded him of...

No, he mustn't think it.

Fate was only teasing. It wouldn't be out of place in Wonderland.

"Rylan?" Ellie murmured, sitting up slowly with sleepy, unfocused eyes trained on him. "Are you all right?"

"I'm fine," he snapped as he pulled his glove back on. "Go back to sleep." He turned away from her, but with an afterthought, he turned back. "Do not address me so familiarly. Your Highness. His Highness. King Rhapsody. Any of the above. Nothing else."

A sultry smirk lifted on her lips, and he found himself powerless to look away. "Then I am Your Sorceressness."

"I'm not calling you that," he scoffed. Reflexively, he glanced toward her right wrist but was vexed when her sleeves covered the entirety of it and then some with the end wrapped around her middle finger, creating a triangle pattern across the back of her hand.

Was she or was she not the other recipient of the unfortunate red heart?

It's nothing, he told himself, taking a calming breath. When he woke the next morning, surely the mark would be gone. It was an illusion. Yes, only an illusion.

"How old are you?" he blurted, but then he stuffed his knuckles into his mouth to keep himself from saying anything more. He didn't want to know anything about her. She was only a means to an end.

Unfortunately, she sat up beside the fire and answered. "Two hundred and fifty."

His gaze traveled up and down her frame, noting her smooth, youthful skin, the lively skip in her dark eyes, the simple grace in which she held herself. Even her auburn curls were voluminous and springy. Nothing about her indicated she was nearly nine times his senior.

"And who was that man inside the Cheshire's illusion?"

Immediately, her expression darkened, the shadows made more prominent by the flickering fire and the wisps of white embers crossing her path. "How did you see him? He was in my mind."

"And so was I." He wanted to wave his yellow rose in front of her face to emphasize his point, but its carcass lay strewn somewhere on the ground.

However, she seemed to grasp his meaning as she scowled. "King Melgren. He's a liar and a snake."

Suddenly, everything clicked in his mind with those few, simple words. Ellie had cursed twelve princesses to dance every night until their feet bled. Revenge? Most likely. On this Melgren fellow. And because Melgren had been accompanied by another woman in the illusion…

Rylan gave her a pointed look. "Let me guess. Melgren Helgren promised you the world in exchange for romantic trysts and then went back on his word when it was no longer convenient for him."

A blush climbed her neck and settled in her cheeks. "That's not what happened. Not exactly. He promised to abdicate the throne so we could run away together. Elope. But he used me for my magic and chose to marry another."

Hmm… Twelve daughters. The king must be fifty years old at the very *least*. Which meant… He laughed. "You've been pining for him for decades."

Ellie picked up a piece of bark and threw it at him. It lightly hit his chest and plopped on the ground. "What do you know? You're so skittish around women that I doubt you even know what love is!"

He waved a nonchalant hand, unfazed. "And you must be the epitome of love yourself, hmm?" Under his breath, he murmured, "Well, you sure know what obsession is, at least."

However, she heard him and threw another piece of bark, this time hitting his chin.

The gall!

He picked up a piece of bark of his own and retaliated, hitting her in the shoulder, holding his chin high and looking down at her. He was the king, and this was his land. Should she hit him again, perhaps she ought to be punished.

Rather than backing down from his haughty expression, she instead grabbed a handful of bark and threw it at him, the little chunks raining down on him like hard sprinklings of rain. He retaliated, and soon bark and dirt flew in all directions, clinging to hair and clothing. Specks of mud followed next until they both started laughing while they threw and dodged and teased.

Mud splatted on one of Ellie's cheeks, and he broke into another fit of laughter, holding his stomach to keep all his jubilance from falling out. She grabbed a handful of mud next and squished it between her fingers, splatting him directly on the forehead, causing her to laugh uncontrollably.

Well, if this was how she wanted to play…

Next, he picked up the kneazle and threatened to throw it at her, but she held up a hand between them. "Stop! Stop. I can recognize when I'm outmatched."

Another chuckle escaped him as he nuzzled the creature against his cheek. "That's what I thought."

"Stop laughing! I'm trying to hate you." Ellie half-heartedly tossed another piece of bark, which hit the tip of his shoe. He only shook his head and grinned.

"All right, all right. Truce." He held out an arm, and they shook air rather than hands. When they settled down again, he brought up his curious thoughts. "Say you break your curse. What then?"

"Countercurse," she replied immediately as she brushed mud and bark from the skirt of her gown. "However, I don't have enough magic to do what I want to do. I must borrow it from somewhere else."

"Mmhmm…" The story was all the same. Revenge, revenge, revenge! Sorceresses were so exciting. "And where do you plan on drawing this power from?"

"A powerful heart, of course. I feel something of its magnitude close by."

Even in the darkness, Ellie noticed Rylan's face growing paler as if all the blood drained from his expression. He swayed where he sat before placing a hand over his mouth as if to stop from retching.

"Rylan?"

Holding up a single finger to ask for a moment, he swallowed and coughed before speaking. "That's *King Rhapsody* to you, witch."

Ellie reeled back as if she were struck across the face. Only moments ago, they'd been playing and laughing. And now? Like putting on a mask, Rylan treated her entirely differently. Even now, he stared moodily into the fire, his eyebrows drawn and his golden eyes reflecting the orange light of the flames. The man reminded her of a cat. One moment, she could be petting a purring feline as it happily flicked its tail and licked her hand, and the next, the creature would bite her and kick up scratches with its back paws despite doing nothing wrong.

That's King Kitty Rhapsody to you.

Her made-up title inspired a laugh that she forced down as a cough. The action attracted his attention, and he opened his mouth as if to say something either witty or stupid, but then the ground shook beneath them. Trees groaned as the tremors tried to pull them from their roots. Birds fluttered from the boughs in a scattering of squawks and flapping wings. The sudden chaos around her almost caused her to miss the way Rylan held a hand to his head, a pained expression on his face. He breathed heavily, his eyes shutting tight.

For a moment, Ellie warred between closing the distance between them to help him through whatever this was and staying put. Especially after the snide way he'd called her a witch.

The tremors left as quickly as they'd come, leaving her own mind reeling. Rylan had said they weren't caused by the giant's footsteps. But then…what were they?

Deciding to distract the king from whatever plagued him, she said, "White, red, black, yellow. There are ten varieties of roses in your garden, but I only know what four of them can do. Care to enlighten me on the rest?"

"Why don't you wait to find out?" he snapped, now rubbing his temples more furiously. "At this rate, I will have used all of them on you, anyway."

A certain vulnerability lingered in his expression, and she decided to press her luck. "When did you discover you were capable of magic? I was seven." At the time, she'd been terrified out of her mind, but now? She was able to laugh about it. "It was at the orphanage. I accidentally gave another girl the face of a pig! It took weeks for the spell to wear off."

He lifted his head and leveled her with a curious stare. "You were an orphan at such a young age?"

She nodded. "My magic made me unadoptable. No one wanted me. Not even the orphanage. I had to learn to take care of myself."

The long, cold nights still haunted her dreams, even a couple hundred years later. Nights huddled beneath a threadbare blanket she'd stolen from a clothesline. Evenings waking up buried in a pile of snow, miraculously still alive when others might have succumbed to the chill. Years of desperately wanting a friend because the lonely life of a sorceress that fate so forcefully placed upon her could not sustain long-lasting relationships.

The reminder created an uncomfortable pit in her stomach, and she forced it away by staring into the fire for a good long time. At least until Rylan finally spoke up.

"All the things I can do…" He glanced somberly at his hands. "I used to be able to do them through touch alone. I quickly discovered it was safer to transfer my power to the roses."

She caught onto the thick emotion in his voice and lifted her hand as if to comfort him but pulled back at the last moment. "What do you mean safer?"

He fell silent for a long time, continuing to stare down at his gloved fingers as the shimmering moonlight dusted over his palms. His stare wavered, his hands trembling. The usually smooth skin between his brows crinkled as if he were experiencing an onslaught of terrible memories.

"I'm tired," he said suddenly, turning a shoulder to her. "It's late."

"Is it?" She glanced toward the moon, watching in awe not for the first time as the moonlight dust sprinkled down like flakes of snow. "Will you hand me your watch?"

This question got him to spin around and stare at her incredulously. "One never gives another their watch. Asking for it is the equivalent of a marriage proposal."

Unbearable heat washed over her face, and she rested her hands on her cheeks to try to hide the raging fluster crawling across her skin. "I-I-I didn't… Y-y-you're not… I-I-I wasn't…"

But then a large grin flashed across his face before he laughed. "I was jesting."

Ugh. She wanted to hit him. And she just might have if he weren't so skittish about people touching him. "You are the worst, do you know that?"

"Pardon?" he gasped, placing a hand against his chest. "And here I thought you wanted to link arms and drink the wedding tea with me."

Not giving her a chance to react to his comment, he pulled out his pocket watch and flipped it open. The numbers spun around in circles, casting a dizzying spell over her head until the world around her seemed to spin and buckle.

With a gasp, her head thumped against a soft pile of semi-damp leaves, kicking up a plume of rot and mildew in its wake. No matter how hard she tried to twist and turn while Rylan loomed over her, she couldn't move her body. Even her tongue refused to work!

"A trick as stale as yesterday's snapper cakes at the Mad Hatter's tea party, darling." He tsked and stared down at her, his silhouette growing darker with every blink of her eyes. "Never stare at someone else's watch. It's bad for your health."

"Ngt nghegan!" she tried to shout, but her words only escaped as a garbled grunt.

The last thing she saw was his pearly grin stretched across his face, bright against the backdrop of the dark forest. "My heart is my own. It does not belong to you."

Before she managed to catch hold of his words and try to make sense of them, darkness pulled her under, and she was helpless against the strength of its mighty grip.

10

Nets Were Made for Catching

The forest was quiet. Almost as if every living creature became silent just so Rylan's guilt could roar mightily in his ears. Leaving Ellie by herself was dangerous, especially while unconscious. But the Heart of Wonderland was more important than her safety.

At least he kept telling himself that. Especially when she'd admitted she wanted to use his heart for her own selfish, revengeful endeavors. She would never have his heart. He refused to let her have it, even just the faintest brush of her fingers. It was his. It didn't belong to anyone else.

Rylan crept forward, his steps light across the forest floor as he moved as silently and deftly as a shadow. The place in his previous vision was somewhere he knew well. On more than one occasion, he and Alice had snuck away from the palace and abandoned his kingly duties to laze about fishing at a lake near a secluded cottage or going on treasure hunts through the woods.

Now he wondered how much of that had been a ruse, how much had been a way to get close enough to him to pluck out his heart like a harpist pulling on their instrument's strings. Never again would he allow someone close enough to trick him. He could not trust anyone.

Especially not Ellie Strife.

At the thought of the sorceress, he moved faster through the winding trees. The pocket watch's hypnotism only lasted a few hours, and he wanted to be tucked safely within his castle by the time she came to.

At last, he spotted the lone cottage in question, something better resembling a crudely built fish shack. Last he saw it, it was sparsely furnished aside from two chairs facing the window, a usually cluttered table, and a clustered wall of fishing rods and a collection of bait.

Glancing around for any sign of another person or creature but finding none, he cautiously approached the shack and reached toward the front door. The hinges creaked open, and he grimaced, glancing around once more.

Peachy Puff squeaked excitedly on his shoulder. He held a finger to his lips, and the little creature bounced up and down before falling silent. Perhaps he should have left the kneazle to guard Ellie.

Hindsight regrets, I suppose.

Trying again, he pushed against the door until it opened wide enough to fit the width of his body. He peeked his head inside, breathing in a puff of the dust floating through the air.

He quietly coughed into his sleeve and braved the first step inside the shack. Everything was just as it should be. Two chairs facing the window. Rows of fishing supplies and stacks of books. Drawers and more drawers stacked along the wall filled with all kinds of silly treasures and important items.

He stepped more fully into the room, each movement careful and calculated. Moonbeams entering through the window illuminated the dust floating through the air. The room was otherwise clean and undisturbed. Quiet and still.

When he found nothing out of the ordinary, he turned in a slow circle but quickly froze.

His face blanched.

A fine, red crystal powder lay scattered across the table, a crimson luster within the fragments. The faintest flicker of light pulsed among the pulverized crystal like the dying embers of a hearth, or rather, a dying heart itself.

"No!" Rylan shouted, sprinting across the room as quickly as his long strides allowed him. Upon closer inspection, he realized this truly was a heart. His own?

No, no, no, no, no. That couldn't be it. It couldn't! But how to explain his vision? It couldn't have been wrong. His heart must be here somewhere.

Denial pulled heavy on every action as he opened drawer after drawer, carelessly spilling their contents across the floor as he searched for his heart. Nails clattered to the floor. Feathers joined the dust floating through the room. One after the other, he threw items and drawers in a mad, crazed state of desperation.

Alice surely thought herself the hero. But what kind of hero toyed with their victims? What kind of hero played little games of hope, only to squash their opponents like candy beneath a shoe?

When he found no such heart, he rushed back toward the table, produced a leather pouch, and began shoving red shards and dust inside. He could still save it. He could still save it!

He reached for a larger chunk of the heart, but the moment he removed it from the table, something clicked under his hand. The ground shifted beneath him, and he gasped when all the air rushed out of him, his feet leaving the floor entirely. His body folded awkwardly with feet higher than his head, his limbs squished uncomfortably together with his arms wrenched painfully over his shoulders, making movement difficult.

His jaw clenched.

Trapped inside a net, his body swung back and forth with the momentum of the capture, the table now out of reach even as he tried to grab the heart fragments to no avail.

Ever so slowly, the last of the light flickered out of the fragments until the shattered crystal dimmed. Dull. Lifeless.

As if Wonderland mourned the terrible loss, another wave of tremors began, shaking the walls and rattling what was left of the drawers. More of his life energy escaped his body, leaving him exhausted and out of breath.

"No..." he whispered as the tremor ceased, and the world around him stopped trembling. He turned his face into his arm and laughed and laughed and laughed until mournful tears cascaded down his face. His body slumped within the net.

"Broken. Woken. Token. Oaken. Misspoken."

A breath shuddered from his lungs, his mind running out of words to rhyme.

His family's legacy… The safety of Wonderland… His own life… It lay in shambles across the table and scattered on the floor. How long did he have left to live? Hours? Days? Weeks? With every passing day, more of the life escaped his soul, and his body became weaker. It wouldn't be long. And now that his heart was destroyed, his death would approach even sooner.

Why would Alice do this? It made no sense to destroy the heart. It was like throwing away one's birthright, one's power, the well-being of an entire kingdom.

In his dejected, mournful state, he hadn't noticed Peachy Puff's absence until now. The little orange fluffball had disappeared, so even the creature couldn't try to get him out of this net before Alice inevitably arrived and did away with him.

At the thought, he struggled against the awkward press of the net, but the more he moved, the more each of his limbs became tangled and trapped. A knife lay in his boot, and a sword at his waist. He managed to reach neither. He just didn't bend that way!

When struggling only exhausted him, he gave up and lay pathetically in the trap like a wild animal waiting for a hunter to return. He should have been more careful. He usually was! Not this time, it seemed. It only took once for stupidity and carelessness to make a fool out of somebody.

Again, he tried to reach for his knife, as it was closer to his fingers than his sword. He reached and stretched, a bead of sweat rolling down his temple at the effort it took to bend his arm at an impossible angle. His legs kicked. His fingers squirmed. Little by little, he managed to maneuver himself closer to his target. Closer. Closer.

"Yes!" he exclaimed as his fingers grasped onto the small hilt of his knife and pulled it free from his boot. But Sir Clumsiness in a Net accidentally nicked the end of the blade against his trousers, causing him to lose his fragile hold on his only means of escape. The knife flew out of his hand and clattered onto the ground beneath him, taunting him with a sheen of silver moonlight reflecting off the metal.

"Drat!"

He slumped even further into despair. He'd held the solution to one of his very many problems in his hand. And now?

"Well…" he murmured to himself as all his previous struggling caused the net to swing him back and forth. "At least this is somewhat relaxing. I think I might set up a hammock in the garden."

Ah, yes. The daylight sun on his face. A cool breeze to ruffle his hair. The scent of sweet roses in the air.

Footsteps crunching on the outside foliage inspired a moment of fear to clog his throat. His entire body stilled. Even his breath moved slowly, quietly in and out of his lungs. Was it Alice? After destroying the Heart of Wonderland, had she returned to finish off the person it once belonged to?

Tension lingered in the air. His limbs tightened with anxiety, and he readied himself for some sort of fight. Even a trapped animal was capable of throwing a punch or two.

The footsteps stopped outside the door. His hands balled into fists. If…if he took off his gloves…

Rylan squeezed his eyes shut, immediately rejecting the idea. He didn't want to use his power to hurt another person, not even if his own life depended on it.

So, he braced himself for the humiliation of capture, closing his eyes only halfway while peeking toward the door beneath his lashes.

A slender boot entered first, followed by a smooth green skirt. Auburn hair. Dark eyes. His eyes snapped open when it wasn't Alice who entered but Ellie. The heat of humiliation still flamed in his cheeks to get caught in such a position. Especially by *her* of all people.

"Well," he said confidently as if he didn't currently have his lower half sitting higher than his upper half. "You caught up quickly."

She took several steps inside the shack and stared up at him with amusement crinkled around her eyes, followed by little Peachy Puff bouncing into the shack behind her. Had the creature led her here?

"I can't decide if you are foolish or brave. No…wait. I can." She lifted an eyebrow and crossed her arms. "Definitely foolish. Do you know how many traps you walked right into? How many you set off? Not including the one currently holding you aloft from the ground."

Rylan scoffed, but the desired effect was lost when one knee touched his ear, and the other was twisted awkwardly above him. "Let me down."

The sorceress tapped a finger against her bottom lip. "I could. But I'm not feeling generous after what you did to me earlier."

"I had my reasons."

"Don't we all?"

After several moments of staring each other down, she grabbed the knife he'd dropped and slowly approached the wall on the opposite side of the room. Within the shadows lay a black rope the same material as the net holding him. She sawed at the rope, and each thread snapped one at a time.

"Wait!" he called. "Let me—"

Gravity swallowed the rest of his words as the last thread of the rope snapped. He plummeted toward the ground and landed with an ungraceful thud.

He spat out a mouthful of net and shoved it aside until it no longer trapped him. "I descrved that," he grunted, climbing to his feet and rubbing his backside.

"Uh huh." She handed back his knife by the hilt and surveyed the room. "My guess is that one of the traps you triggered pulverized the heart."

He released a long, shaky breath. There was no choice but to tell her, to try to place some trust in her. "Can you tell if it's mine?"

"Wouldn't you know?"

"Would I?"

She rolled her eyes and pushed past him to stand in front of the table. "Only someone with magical talent possesses hearts such as these. Crystal-like and strong rather than soft and fragile. A magic-wielder can survive without their heart for only so long, but if someone were to destroy it… You would already be dead."

"Just make sure is all I'm asking."

Ellie leaned over the red fragments and dust, inspecting it closely without touching it. After several long moments, she straightened. "No, it does not belong to you."

Her condescending tone made him believe she only pretended to check to appease him.

"Then who does it belong to?"

"A very unfortunate person. I can surmise nothing else from these fragments. But my guess?" She lifted her gaze to meet his eye. "Whoever did this planned to scare you. Or capture you. Probably both."

"I gathered that," he grumbled, now understanding his previous vision. Had Ellie gone to the shack with him, she would have noticed the traps, and the heart would have survived. However, it hadn't been his heart on the line but someone else who was powerful enough to attract the sorceress's interest.

When the sorceress remained silent for a beat too long, he lifted his gaze to find her staring at him. "So, *King Rhapsody*… Are you going to tell me the entire truth?"

11

Obsession Turns The Heart Dark

Rylan's mouth turned downward into a stubborn pout. He crossed his arms, lifted his nose, and turned a cold shoulder to her. "Why should I? You wanted to use this heart for your own means, after all."

Internally, Ellie sighed as she rubbed her suddenly aching temples. Talking to him was like riding in the back of a cart and an obstacle lay ahead in the road. But rather than the driver warning her to hold on, he stopped the cart so suddenly for her to lose her balance and jerk into the side wall and hit her head and lose her ever-living sanity. What was a worse punishment? The Cheshire's ramblings or the whiplash the Mad King often gave her?

"If you had told me you suspected it was your own heart, I may have left it alone."

"May?" he scoffed. "*May*? Hmm? So, there was still a chance you might have taken it."

She shrugged unapologetically. Her conundrum was more important than his own. "However, might I point out that this situation could very well have ended up differently should it have actually been your heart. You can't just rush into a situation like this."

The man's ears turned red, but the stubborn cross of his arms remained. The tension in his shoulders loosened after a few moments, but he was still turned away from her. "She didn't used to be like this."

"Who?"

"Alice."

Ellie paused for a moment, glancing over his face but finding nothing to betray his expression. "A paramour?"

Rylan spun around and placed a hand against his chest with a gasp. "A paramour? Who do you think I am?"

She rubbed her temples again after yet another whiplash. "All right. If not that, then what?"

His gaze was far away as he turned his golden pocket watch around in his hand. "I once called her a friend. Just two little orphaned children rediscovering the world together after the first one betrayed us."

That makes three, including me. It wasn't entirely uncommon to lose one's parents in a harsh world, but the similarity put her on guard. Sorceresses believed it only took three similarities to reveal that fate was involved. She didn't want to believe fate had any hand in bringing her here when she needed to return to the upper world with her magic intact.

Continuing, Rylan said, "And then *she* betrayed *me* by stealing my heart, the Heart of Wonderland might I add, while my guard was down."

Silence.

"And?" she asked.

"And what? That's it."

All right, that did it. She needed a nap to reset her addled brain.

Unable to stand staying a minute longer in the shack, she led Rylan outside and around what remained of the traps he hadn't already set off. Only when they entered the forest did he scoop up Peachy Puff and take the lead back to the castle.

Ellie stepped over a pile of fallen leaves and ducked under the branch Rylan held aloft for her. "If you had been honest from the beginning, I would have approached the situation differently."

"How?" he asked, absently petting the demon-creature as if it hadn't very recently tried to take a bite out of them.

"It can only be done successfully by a powerful sorceress," she said, not wanting to give the king any ideas that he could try it by himself. She'd lose her leverage otherwise. "I would capture a white rabbit to lead us to where Alice is hiding your heart."

"How would the rabbit manage such a feat?"

She wagged a finger back and forth at him. "Nuh uh uh. A trade. For real this time. The Heart of Wonderland for the knowledge of how to get my magic back."

He stomped forward, and she cringed at how much noise he was making. What if he attracted some other nefarious beast even more terrifying than a kneazle?

"Why do you need your magic so badly?" he demanded. "You're better off without it. Trust me."

She tripped over a fallen branch, quickly righting herself before trying to analyze the disdain laced through his words. Was he unhappy about wielding magic himself? But his was so powerful! The things he could do with it if he only had a mind to do so.

Her thoughts swirled darkly on the upper realm and the people there, and she admitted angrily, "It's for revenge on the man who broke my heart."

"Ah, yes. The dancing princesses curse. I remember now." He glanced at her over his shoulder with an air of arrogance about him. "Soooo…you want revenge on the man who hurt you. Isn't he, what, eighty years old by now?"

She gritted her teeth. "That's not the point! And he's not eighty. Closer to sixty now."

"Same difference. The point is that he's moved on times forty years, no? You should move on as well. Find someone else to wreak your obsession on." He giggled to himself as if he thought himself hilarious. He absolutely was not.

"I'm not obsessed," she replied stubbornly, arms crossed.

He lifted his brows. "No? I would consider cursing twelve innocent girls to dance every night for weeks or months or years or however long just because of their father is pushing that obsession just a little itty bit too far."

"What do you know? You know nothing of the situation."

He clicked his tongue, his gaze briefly darting to her collarbone. "Oh, I see now. You've obsessed for so long that your heart turned black. If you're not careful, even that level of resentment can kill a sorceress."

"What do you know?" she spat again, gesturing to him. "You don't even have a heart."

He sucked a sharp breath between his teeth and placed a hand against his chest. "Must you wound me so?"

Ugh! Where was a nap when she needed one? Just dealing with the King of Hearts for a single conversation was enough to vex even the most patient of souls.

Despite wanting to brush the matter under the rug, an inexplicable need to argue her case arose within her. The words simply burst out of her mouth. "You don't even know what love is! You have no woman in your life as far as I can tell, and you must treat your friends terribly! Even I wouldn't go so far as using my powers against the few people I have called friends throughout my life."

Rylan's eye twitched as if she'd struck a nerve. "And you must be the epitome of love? Hmm?" And then he said under his breath, "Well, you sure know what obsession is, at least."

Ellie furiously rubbed at her temples, the headache growing stronger with each passing minute. She wanted to drop this matter. But perhaps he'd also struck a nerve with her.

After a pause, she asked, "You really think I'm obsessed?"

"If you have to ask the question…"

He grinned slyly at her. She almost slapped him. This time, she dropped the subject, not wanting to get into a wit war with someone far more talented with words than herself.

Just when she thought another hour or two waited for her on the trail leading back to the castle, they rounded a bend, and it waited for them just ahead. She placed a hand to her forehead as she tried to make sense of the short journey back. It had taken a couple hours plus a good chasing to end up at the shack. And minutes to return? The logic of traveling made little to no sense in the lower world. Part of her wanted to ask Rylan. But the stronger part of her didn't want to exacerbate her headache.

She let the issue go. For now.

On their way back to the castle in the darkness, with only specks of moonbeams to light their way, she realized Rylan had been quiet for a while. That was never a good sign.

She turned to find his eyes far away, his expression deep in thought. But the furrow of his brows indicated the thoughts weren't necessarily pleasant.

Don't ask, she warned herself. *It's not my business, and I don't care.*

But the pitiful downturn of his lips snagged at something inside her, and she couldn't help but ask anyway. "You look troubled."

"Mm," he agreed, turning his head the slightest bit to look her way. "I am simply amused by your sorceressly antics. But you speak of me like I'm some sort of villain."

"Well…" She grinned and gave him a pointed stare. "If you check the boxes…"

"What boxes? There are no boxes to check!"

Were they really starting up another fight? Fine then.

She ticked off on her fingers, "You siphon energy from other people. You force others to catch feelings for you. You force others to speak the truth against their will. You manipulate and manipulate some more, and you don't feel even an ounce of remorse."

"Look in the mirror, love. How are you any better than me? Besides, I do what I do for the sake of the kingdom."

"For the kingdom's sake? Or your own?"

Rylan's fists clenched at his side, his arms shaking. His eyes flashed a brilliant, angry gold, and without another word, he spun around and strode back toward the castle on his own, the black cape draped over one shoulder fluttering lightly in the breeze. When he wore mostly black, she quickly lost sight of him in the shadows.

A surprising stab of regret burned through her as she stared after where he'd disappeared. She was no saint. She'd done questionable things in her life. Besides, what he did was not any of her business. She just…didn't like this feeling churning inside of her after everything the Mad King had said.

With an ache pounding hard enough against her skull that she was convinced no amount of medicine could cure, she stalked grumpily through the garden and toward the servants' quarters.

The sooner she left Wonderland, the better.

12

A Daring Maze Rescue

Several days passed, and rather than feeling energized over the hope of finding his heart soon, Rylan's body became weaker.

Each time Wonderland quaked, he lost a bit more of his strength.

Citizens in the kingdom quietly voiced their apprehension over the consistent tremors. More than one of his friends approached with concern over his well-being. And that…well…it created a pit of guilt in his stomach as he recalled Ellie's words from days prior.

"You siphon energy from other people. You force others to catch feelings for you. You force others to speak the truth against their will. You manipulate and manipulate some more, and you don't feel even an ounce of remorse."

He stared hard at the black rose he twiddled between his fingers. While he used to enjoy breathing in its lovely fragrance, he couldn't bring himself to lift the flower to his nose, to inhale the powerful dark magic boiling within.

Until now, he'd siphoned energy from others to sustain himself to keep Wonderland afloat. But now? Guilt was his constant companion.

One after the other, he absently snapped the thorns off the rose until the stem lay bare, and little pocked scars marked the living weapon as useless. This entire situation was useless, anyway. Before he'd even cut the rose from its bush, the petals had wilted, and not from lack of water or care.

They were dying.

Because he was dying.

He reached for another black rose within a vase on the table. But just like the other, he began snapping off thorn after thorn until it lay bare. The words Ellie had struck him with still left him reeling. What right did he have to take from others without their permission if only to keep himself alive? How was this any different than what had happened with his mother? Except, rather than accidentally taking all her life force at once, he was taking little by little from his subjects.

"Mother," he whispered, rubbing his aching chest with his fingers. Oh, how he missed her fiercely. Her smile and her laughter. The silliness that had always kept him in stitches as a young boy.

He missed her smile the most. Like drops of sunshine rain all gathered in the glow of a face. And he'd taken that light away with a single touch of his hand.

Pushing the black flowers aside, he realized he couldn't deliver them to his intended recipients. He could no longer stomach the idea.

And when had he started to grow a conscience?

Ridiculous sorceress, he grumbled in his mind. He doubted she had a conscience of her own at all. So why had she thrust one upon himself?

The achy fatigue in his body made him feel downright sorry for his own situation. Therefore, he picked one of the well-read books from his drawing room shelf, sat at the table, and opened the pages. The familiar must of old parchment greeted his nose and settled his rising anxiety.

Patience. He must practice patience.

He flipped page after page, engrossed in the mad ramblings of previous kings of Wonderland. He enjoyed books about history or the memoirs of those farther down his ancestral line. He especially paid heed to the ramblings of his own father tacked onto the previously blank pages at the end of this particular book, written in the man's own handwriting. He was one of the most insane people to have ever existed. It was amazing!

Movement outside the window drew his attention, and his chest tightened when he recognized the auburn curls and light spatter of freckles of the person they belonged to.

Ellie Strife bent over a small portion of the herb garden, her finger hovering over one plant and then another before she made her selection. She used a pair of pruning shears to cut a sprig of this and a sprig of that, her expression focused and thoughtful.

He couldn't help but stare, his gaze roaming over her in appreciation. The sorceress was…well, beautiful. He hadn't cared to notice before. But he noticed now. He liked her hair and her face and her eyes. The way she was shaped. How she was one of the very few people willing to speak their mind around him. He liked being chastised by her. He liked when she was angry, too. He found her ire rather charming.

Yes, she's quite pretty, he admitted to himself, watching her place sprigs of herbs inside a small basket slung over one arm.

At this point, he still didn't know whether she possessed the accompanying mark on her wrist to match his own. But… Perhaps it didn't even matter. She was pretty to look at, but he'd never consider taking a risk with anyone, even a sorceress, by exposing them to the deadly power swirling within his core.

"I haven't felt a tremor in a few hours," someone commented beside him.

"Jumping Jabberwackys!" Rylan yelped, the fright nearly making him visit the grave too early as he placed a hand against his chest. He turned to find Gideon Glimmer sitting in the chair to his left. "When did you get here?"

"I've been here the entire time. Didn't you see me?"

"Obviously, no."

"Ah." A twinkle sparkled in the man's eyes. "Too busy looking at other things."

Rylan scoffed and rolled his eyes, finally tearing his attention away from the sorceress. "I was admiring the garden, is all."

"Mmhmm. Very beautiful flowers down there." Another twinkle in his eye. Rylan chose to ignore the insinuation.

"What brings you to the drawing room?" Rylan asked as he picked up his book once again. Only after a few moments did he realize he held it upside down and turned it back around again.

"To chat." Gideon leaned his arms against the table and glanced at him knowingly, instantly making Rylan suspicious. What did he know? How much did he know? "About the tremors."

Rylan gritted his teeth and turned his head away. "They're only temporary. Wonderland is fine."

"I'm not worried about Wonderland. I'm worried about you."

Rylan stared at his friend in shock, who stared back with a furrow between his brows, made more prominent by the monocle he wore in one eye. Slowly, Rylan lowered his book, a frown forming on his face.

"I'm fine." But even the tone of his own voice did nothing to convince himself. Gideon likely saw through him as well.

Gideon patted the top of his arm. "What can we do to help?"

"We?"

His friend nodded toward the doorway. Rylan's next swallow snagged on his throat as he noticed his group of friends lingering on the opposite side of the room. Piper Pixiewing fluttered her shimmering wings. Luna Larkspur waved at him with hands made of branches and leaves. Julian Jester. Thaddeus Thimble. Clio Clockchime.

Emotion caught in his chest, and he found it difficult to keep himself steady when faced with all their support. Yes, they were his friends. But he'd still held the weight of the kingdom on his own shoulders. He'd faced hardship after hardship alone, and he'd thought he'd have to face it alone again.

But...

What if he wasn't as alone as he'd thought? A warmth blossomed inside him at the realization. These people, his friends, were here to help. They cared about the kingdom. They cared about *him*.

Clearing his throat, he spoke to everyone at once. "We need a white rabbit." Because apparently, finding a white rabbit was almost as impossible as taking a clean breath underwater. "Does anyone have any ideas?"

Luna Larkspur grew an arm-length taller, her obsidian black eyes blinking quickly. "I have friends in the forest. We'll search there."

"Great. Also, Sorceress Ellie could use some help in the apothecary."

Piper Pixiewing fluttered her wings, the movement casting pink and green light across the walls of the drawing room. "Leave it to me."

Rylan nodded gratefully, the faintest bit of hope beginning to shine down on him like a ray of afternoon light. "I also need help maintaining morale between our subjects."

This time, Gideon Glimmer spoke up as he turned his monocle around his fingers blindingly fast. "I have a few ideas. I'll take care of it." And then he grinned. "And Clio as well. What's a party without a little Clockchime?"

Everyone fell silent. Rylan quickly became uncomfortable beneath their stares. "Well?" He waved a nonchalant hand to dismiss them. "Go do your things. Tick tock. Mind the clock!"

They didn't move. Rather, each of his friends knelt to one knee in fealty to not only their friend, but to their king. His emotions caught in his throat all over again, and he found himself unable to hold their gazes. He glanced to the side while crossing his arms.

"We were there," Gideon said, bowing his head. "At the unbirthday celebration with Alice. We know she stole your heart. We know you're dying because of it. If you would just…" He blew out a long breath as if unsure how to continue.

Julian Jester's hundred rings flashed beneath the nearby lantern light as he dipped his head to speak. "We're offering our energy to you, to help you overcome this. The kingdom needs you. You can't falter now."

Rylan's hands balled into fists as he fixed his stare on the wall to his right. "I'm not sure what you mean by that."

Gideon laughed, drawing Rylan's attention to him and the others behind him. "You're sneaky, Your Highness. But not sneaky enough for me. We know you've been stealing energy from others. We understand why. You don't feel like you have much choice."

Guilt pressed down on his shoulders, and he dropped his hands to his sides. "I'm sorry. I should never have… I never took from any of you."

"We know. But we are willing to give, regardless."

As he stared back at Gideon, in particular, he felt torn. Although the other man looked his same age, he was at least four times older, and he'd been around even since his birth. Even since his mother had died as well.

How much did they know about his powers?

Glancing between the lot of them, he realized they knew enough.

He shook his head and held his hands behind his back. He refused to use the black roses again, and to take energy from them, even when offered, he'd have to touch their bare skin. He could kill them. He couldn't risk it.

"I will not take from anyone, but..." He glanced out the window, the corner of his mouth flickering into an almost smile when he spotted Ellie down below, her curiosity seeming to get the better of her as she entered the hedge maze and got lost within the space of a few seconds. "I value your support. Let's work on finding Alice before the entire kingdom falls apart."

His friends nodded and quickly left the room, leaving Gideon and himself by themselves. A comfortable silence descended upon the room as they watched Ellie's familiar silhouette move below in the maze.

He chuckled to himself, crossing his arms as he watched her flit back and forth around the hedges, growing visibly more frustrated with each passing minute. Each time she turned a corner, the hedges shifted and closed the way behind her.

Too hilarious! He enjoyed watching people get lost in the maze, but he found it even more amusing when it was her.

He released a sigh and lowered his arms, sharing a knowing look with Gideon. "I suppose I should go and rescue her."

"Leaving her for a few more minutes won't hurt."

Rylan laughed, his entire being so much lighter after his friends had taken some of his burdens from him. "True. Besides, the longer I leave her there, the happier she'll be to see me."

He coughed when he realized what he'd just said. She was a means to an end. That was all.

Shaking his head, he chuckled when she ran around the corner only to face a dead end. "Really?! Did no one warn her to stay out of the maze?" His grin grew wider. "Oh, right. That was my job."

Gideon Glimmer returned his grin with one of his own before Rylan strode out of the drawing room, making sure to pull his gloves down farther to conceal the black spade mark on his wrist.

The great thing about getting lost...

It was fun to get lost in pairs.

13

Stairway to Nowhere

This infuriating maze!

Ellie stomped down a path with tall hedges on either side of her, trying to find the exit. Her curiosity tonight or this afternoon of *whatever blasting time it was!*—it had been her downfall.

Sure, Ellie. Let's enter a hedge maze in the heart of Wonderland. What a great idea! What could possibly go wrong?

She wasn't sure how much time had passed. At least an hour. And she was still stuck in this maze with no way out. Even when she tried to backtrack, she'd quickly lost her way.

When she ran into yet another dead end, she turned back around, only to find that the way was blocked as if the path had closed behind her. Was that what this was? A maze that continuously changed directions and made it impossible to find the exit? Whoever thought this was a good idea?

She groaned out loud and kicked the hedge, only for the walling plant to suck her entire foot in as if trying to eat her. Angrily, she tugged and tugged, each attempt more desperate than the last. When she thought her leg was good and stuck forever, the hedge suddenly spit out her foot, and she cried out as she stumbled backward and crashed into something that made an "oof!" sound as she fell.

She grunted and pushed up on her elbows, only to find herself nose to nose with the King of Madness himself. His gold eyes stared back at her in shock, the man completely silent. She was no better, as her mouth moved yet no words escaped. How was he impossibly more handsome close up?

"How dare you touch me!" Rylan roared when the shock dissipated from his eyes, replaced by anger. She tried to untangle herself from him, but the toe of her shoe was caught on his boot. "I ought to dangle you from a rope as a meal for the jabberwacky for such impudence. You—!"

He released another "oof!" as she crashed back down on him, this time elbowing him in the ribs. She pushed herself up again, but this time her hands used his chest as leverage. She shouldn't have been surprised when she realized he was nothing but hard muscle.

"Get off me!" Rylan shouted, rolling over so she fell to the ground rather than using his hands to push her away. He climbed to his feet and dusted himself off, wearing a deep scowl on that pretty face of his.

Before he had a chance to try to sentence her to something completely outrageous for her folly, she cut in, "What are you doing here? How did you find me?"

He grumpily pointed to a castle window overlooking the garden. "I watched you run yourself silly until I couldn't stand it any longer. I came to your rescue, but I'm not sure I feel in the rescuing mood anymore."

Embarrassment flamed in her cheeks, followed by a strange warmth inside her chest. It was almost as if her black heart transitioned into a dark shade of gray.

No…

It was impossible.

She ignored the feeling and pushed past him, purposefully coming close enough to nearly brush against his arm. He recoiled from her and grimaced with a ghastly expression, and she couldn't help but laugh at him. Oh, the horror of a woman's touch!

Just for the fun of it, she fake-lunged at him. He gasped and flinched, the ghost almost seeming to leave his body.

"Rude!" he cried, giving her another scowl. "You're fired! Fired, you hear me?"

"And losing your only chance at finding your heart?"

Rylan blew a long breath from his mouth, his black curls ruffling with the light breeze. "The things I must put up with! Woe is me."

He led the way, and as she followed a step behind him, she placed a fist against her mouth and chuckled silently. When she first met him, he'd been exasperating. He still was. But she was beginning to understand his moods and shenanigans.

To some degree.

As they traveled through the dark maze with the moonbeams raining over them like silver dewdrops, she turned to him and gestured to the tall hedges around them. "What is the point of this? The magic is unfair, and it's infuriatingly easy to get lost."

"That's the best part about it!" he laughed, his mood shifting entirely. "It's unsolvable. How fun."

"Fun?" she squeaked. "Aren't you the least bit concerned about getting lost in here? Forever? What if we never make it back out?"

"Ellie, Ellie, Ellie." He clicked his tongue and shook his head. "To find your way, sometimes you must lose yourself."

"That makes no sense!"

"Doesn't it, though? If you always get to where you're going, you'll never arrive at the right destination."

She pinched the bridge of her nose, feeling another headache coming on. She should be used to these headaches by now, but Rylan somehow found new and improved ways of twisting the mind.

"Anyways," she sighed, glancing over to find him watching the stars overhead rather than the path in front of him. For a moment, he appeared peaceful. Thoughtful.

Beautiful.

There was a certain gentle beauty about him in the gold of his eyes, the smooth texture of his skin, the piercing angle of his eyebrows. He was unlike anything she'd seen before in her own land. Poets and musicians would have trampled over each other just to write sonnets and musical pieces about his handsome appearance. If they could cast aside the confusing things he said and his ability to switch moods at the drop of a mad hat.

"Anyways...what?" he asked, giving her a playful smirk. "Did you lose your train of thought?"

Ugh.

She quickly glanced away from him, heat rising to her face and escaping her ears as non-existent steam. If he ever found out about some of those thoughts...

Quickly, she changed the subject, "I have not found a white rabbit yet, but I'm working on it. Either way, you promised to tell me how to break my curse."

They turned around a corner to find a lone bench covered in pink, flowering vines. But they continued forward beneath a black arch and through a tunnel of hedges.

"As a sorceress, I'm surprised you don't know the answer."

"Just tell me." And when his eyebrows started to pull together to form a scowl, she added, "Please."

He pushed aside soft, hanging willows to allow her to go through before him, only to be met by a fork in the hedges. He closed his eyes and turned around in a circle three times before choosing the path on the right.

"The answer is as simple as this. If exile was your punishment, then ex-exile is your cure."

And cue the next headache. "What are you even talking about?"

"Is it really so hard to understand, darling?" He sighed exasperatedly and planted his hands on his hips, staring at the sky. "You sorceresses are always looking for more power to get your magic back. And it fails every time. That's because you are looking in the wrong place." He held up two fingers. "Either, one, you kill your caster. Or, two, you return to the place you were cursed. Simple as that."

She shuddered. "I wouldn't call killing someone simple."

"Of course, it is!" He mimicked swinging something through the air. "Just the right angle of the ax and wham! Deed is done."

She stared at him, not sure if he was serious. With him, one never knew. He had shown the last gardener mercy by sending him to the caterpillar fields. But what about the previous sorceresses he had run into? And when they had met, he'd sentenced her to losing her head.

However... Now that she understood Wonderland a little bit more each day, and as she got to know Rylan's mischievous attitude, she realized "Off with her head!" might not have actually meant what she thought it had. Or had it?

"And what about me?" she asked, voicing those thoughts. "You sentenced me to lose my head." She dragged a hand across her throat.

"Did I?" He raised his brow. "Or did I sentence you to the Cheshire's mad rambling until you completely lost your mind? But you ended up running into its territory anyway. You completed your sentence all on your own! What an exciting twist."

"I…" She trailed off, rubbing her forehead when a sudden ache throbbed in her temples. Small details and turns of phrases… The things that came out of Rylan's mouth should no longer surprise her, but he still managed to catch her off guard.

The maze opened into what appeared to be a small courtyard with a variety of plants, flowers, arches, and benches. Rylan took a seat on a stone bench beneath a red-flowering, willow-like tree. Hesitantly, she joined him. Although she wanted to leave the maze altogether, she didn't find his company too terrible…

He plucked one of the flowers and twirled it between his fingers. "What luck!" he said, inhaling the flower before presenting it to her. "Fizzleblooms only open their petals once a year. What a beauty they are."

After a moment of uncertainty, she accepted the flower, careful not to touch him, and inhaled the sweet fragrance. A faint tingle touched her nose and lips. She marveled at what magical properties it might contain and only wished to study it further. If she wasn't in such a dire situation, she might have asked to dissect it in the apothecary.

A faint shimmer in the sky caught her attention, and her eyes widened when she spotted a staircase seemingly made of translucent rainbow light. It started somewhere on the ground and climbed into the sky, disappearing from view as if it had no end.

"What is that?" she whispered in awe. One moment, the stairs seemed invisible, but the next, the moonlight caught onto it and rippled a rainbow of color across its surface.

He followed her gaze. "It's the stairway to nowhere. Just when you think there's no end in sight, you're a quarter of the way there!"

"But…where does it lead?"

"Wherever you're going."

She released an exasperated sigh. "Rylan—"

"Eh eh eh." He wagged a finger at her. "King Rhapsody to you."

"King Rhapsody," she tried again with another sigh. "That makes no sense."

He clicked his tongue. "Upper dwellers never understand."

For several long moments, they both gazed up at the magnificent sky with its rainbow stairs and sparkling moonbeams. Wonderland was…beautiful. For several peaceful minutes, she experienced a heart lacking hurt and disdain and anger. Trapped within a hedge maze with seemingly no way out, she'd never felt more free.

Which was silly, considering her magic was trapped with no way out but to end her caster's life or return to Melgren's castle. The thought filled her with discomforting unease.

Slowly, she turned her head until she glanced at Rylan, who wore a sad expression as he gazed up at the stars. What was on his mind?

"You know…" She bit her lip, wondering if she could continue. If she *should* continue. "There are ways to control your magic without living with the fear of hurting others. If you'd like to learn."

Rylan grimaced, quickly standing and turning his back to her while brushing off his sleeve. "Who said anything about hurting others? I don't fear my magic. Anyways, let's get out of here. I've had enough of hedge mazes to last a week."

Ellie followed several steps behind, staring at the back of his head when his face was turned away while also obscured in shadows. She'd never really cared about the Mad King. But now... She couldn't help but notice that he was plenty more complicated than she'd previously believed.

Surprisingly, Rylan led them out of the hedge maze as if he were on a simple stroll around a riverwalk. When they exited the maze and entered the garden, Ellie's heart climbed to her throat in shocking despair. The roses!

Many of the flowers had wilted as if they were thirsting for water. Many others looked brittle to the touch, like they might crumble to pieces with the faintest brush of her finger. What had she done? She thought she'd been taking good care of the roses, but this...

She was in big trouble.

She imagined a noose around her neck or another bout of exposure to the Cheshire Cat's terrible illusions. Rylan would never forgive her for this. She might as well kiss her own life goodbye.

But as Rylan's gaze passed over the garden, his expression only grew solemn rather than angry.

"I can explain!" Ellie cried, desperate to save her own life in any way she could. Even if she had to throw herself at his feet and beg until the sun eventually appeared in the sky.

However, the king appeared unfazed.

"Just water them," he murmured somberly. "I'm sure they'll perk right up."

Without another word, he turned on his heel and melted into the shadows.

Ellie approached the black roses she once feared and touched the ebony petals. Once soft, they now crumbled from her touch like dried herbs pressed into powder beneath her pestle.

What was happening to the roses?

And even more concerning…

What was happening to King Rhapsody?

14

THE SORCERESS LEARNS TO DANCE

"So, what is this for again?" Piper Pixiewing fluttered her iridescent gossamer wings, hovering a hand's width off the ground. Just a head shorter than Ellie herself, she leaned over the table, watching with rapt interest as Ellie grounded up magical herbs inside a mortar within the apothecary.

Ellie couldn't help but smile to herself at the camaraderie and companionship between them. If Ellie had had any intention of staying, they might have become good friends.

"I have to get creative when I don't have my magic," she grunted, putting her weight into mixing the herbs. "I'm making a tracking spell. Once we combine it with something that belongs to Alice, the white rabbit should be able to guide us to her location."

"Ah." Her wings fluttered thoughtfully. "I see. And why use a rabbit?"

"Because they have useful magical properties. Not only are they closely associated with the push and pull of time, but they are also incredible guides."

"Hmm." Piper fluttered closer until she nearly stuck her nose directly into the mortar.

Ellie laughed and shifted it away from her. "Unless you want to live with some adverse effects from the magic in here, I advise you to keep your distance."

"Oh, fine." The pixie looked entirely put out as she sat on the edge of the table, her wings drooping behind her. Several minutes of silence passed while Ellie measured ingredients, her brows scrunched with concentration.

When Piper spoke next, she jumped, forgetting she wasn't alone. "So…" the other woman said slyly. "Rylan, hmm?"

"What about him?" The dark gray heart beating inside her warmed a shade lighter, though she had no idea why.

"We all saw you two in the maze together. You both looked rather cozy."

Laughter erupted from her mouth, finding Piper's words amusing as she envisioned all of Rylan's friends with their faces nosily pressed against the glass of the window to spy on them.

She added a sprig of timberleaf extract and stirred it in with the other ingredients before lifting her head. "Are you talking about before or after he chewed my head off several times with his spitting words? Also, does no one have anything better to do than watch me flounder from that window?"

"No," Piper giggled. Her laughter reminded Ellie of the mischievous water sprites that lived in the upper realm in the River Bryn. "Not if it involves Rylan. He's hardly so much as glanced in a woman's direction for as long as I've known him. But he can't seem to stay away from *you*."

She rolled her eyes while carefully adding the concoction into a small vial. All she needed now was something that once belonged to Alice as well as a white rabbit. Unless...

She drummed her fingers against the table as she realized she could also go in another direction. On one hand, they could locate Alice and possibly kill two birds with one stone. On the other hand, they could directly locate Rylan's heart. It was a more complicated spell, one she might not be able to achieve with her magic. It was far more difficult to find objects over people, but it was a slim possibility.

Piper jutted out her bottom lip in a pout. "You're ignoring me. I said—"

"Yes, yes, he sure does like to torment me with headaches. I'm not sure why all of you are reading too much into it."

"I'm just saying... Maybe you should dress up for the ball tonight."

"Hah." Her focus was already diverted as she placed several potted plants beside the window. Unfortunately, the plants would receive no sunlight for the time being. Where was that giant when she needed it?

"Clio Clockchime throws the best parties. You don't want to miss out."

"And do what? Hug the corner like a wallflower? Not interested."

Uncertainty crept up in her chest, a frown forming at the thought. She kept her face turned toward the window to hide her expression, fussing over the plants in her care. Yes, she'd cursed princesses to dance until their feet bled. But she'd never once danced herself. She wasn't that kind of woman who got a happy fairytale ending and danced with lighthearted laughter until the break of dawn.

Fate would never be so kind.

Besides, the sooner she found this Heart of Wonderland, the sooner she could return to the upper world and finish her plight for revenge once and for all.

She chewed on her cheek, staring down at a fuzzy leaf between her fingers. She could leave now. Sneak away while everyone was distracted at the ball.

However, she risked running into a similar situation to the one she'd endured after first arriving in Wonderland. She had no desire to be chased by some strange creature with sharp claws and teeth. She might not find herself so lucky the next time to escape almost unscathed.

Ridiculous. Wonderland held her captive simply by her lack of knowledge alone. The only way to leave was to give King Rhapsody exactly what he wanted first.

"So…I'll see you tonight, then?" Piper asked with the same sly tone as before.

"No. I'm too busy in the apothecary." She opened her hand, startled to find the fuzzy leaf crushed within her palm. Although she certainly was no gardener, she was a sorceress who often used plants in her potions and poultices. They were a precious commodity not to be wasted.

If she could keep them alive for longer than a week.

Piper Pixiewing flitted in front of her, blocking her view of the plants in the window with her large wings. "But Rylan specifically asked if you were going. I don't want to disappoint him by telling him no."

A strange flutter came to life within her chest, and her eyebrows furrowed at the unfamiliar sensation. She rubbed a hand beneath her collarbone and frowned. "He wouldn't have asked such a question. You can stop pretending."

"But I'm not." Her tinkling laughter flew across the room before she settled in an alcove near the top of the room with a window overlooking the gardens outside. "He certainly has a no-touch rule with everyone around him. But I wouldn't be surprised if he made an exception for you."

Ellie snorted, thinking back to the hedge maze and how he'd run scared from her touch. It was a shame he was so frightened by his own magic. He could otherwise become so powerful that he wouldn't need a sorceress to track down his own heart for him.

"We'll see," she hummed, trying to appease the other woman for now. Her main goal was to return home. She must place all other distractions aside.

But several hours later when she returned to her room, she stopped short when she found a red ball gown waiting for her, splayed out over her bed. Shock rooted her feet to the floor as she stared at the masses of red fabric as if they might leap out at her and drag her into their crimson depths. But underneath her layers of shock...

A sense of overpowering awe overcame her as she dared to trail her fingers over the unbelievably soft fabric, the ruffles across the shoulders, the deep red corset. Never in her life had she touched such a beautiful, luxurious dress, let alone wear one.

There had to be some mistake. She was not a princess. She was a sorceress. A witch. A woman who had always lived in the shadows rather than strut about in the sunlight.

But as she spotted a single note with only three words written across the parchment, she knew she wasn't mistaken.

For Her Sorceressness.

That was all the note said, but she immediately knew who it was from. King Rylan Rhapsody. Truly, why did he care whether she attended a silly party? And why must he bother with delivering a silly, gorgeous, breathtaking gown?

She recalled Piper's words from earlier.

Rylan specifically asked if you were going. I don't want to disappoint him by telling him no.

For a long few moments, she debated between staying in her room to finish up her work and going to a ball she had no business attending. But this time…

She didn't have to sneak in. She didn't have to dole out a curse. She could just arrive in a beautiful gown and…

And then what? She wasn't entirely sure what happened at a regular ball where she *wasn't* threatening to enact some curse or another.

After a long sigh, she lifted the mountains of skirts and twirled with the dress in her arms. *Fine. I'll go.*

But if Rylan so much as laughed at her for wearing something so large and frivolous, she was leaving first thing.

Someone knocked on her door. Her eyebrows furrowed in confusion. No one had ever visited her room before, so who could it be?

She opened the door, only for her heart to shoot to her throat in shock when faced with Piper Pixiewing, Cleo Clockchime, and Luna Larkspur with huge grins on their faces and a variety of hairbrushes, pins, and ribbons in their hands.

Lovely, she sighed in exasperation. Was it too late to run?

Forget about being a wallflower. Ellie hardly had the courage to step into the ballroom in the first place!

She wasn't sure why her stomach twisted into knots or the reason her heart fluttered as if she'd missed a stair or two. All she knew was the ballgown she wore was bigger than any dress she'd ever donned, and her usual mess of curls had been tamed into something beautiful and elegant.

Ellie eyed a group of women across the room from where she lingered by the doorframe. They were all humans or other creatures she had yet to encounter, all wearing something to make them truly shine. She recognized those like Luna Larkspur crafted of branches and leaves, and others similar to Felix Flamewood, half-caterpillar, half-human.

Most ball goers looked like humans but with a unique flare. For example, one man in a black suit had several sets of arms and a few extra eyes on his face. Another woman wore bangled jewelry all the way up to her elbows, her skin transitioning through several different shades of color. First red, then pink, blue, gold, and back to pink.

Elegant music drew her attention to the musicians playing flutes and stringed instruments in the corner of the enormous room, their fluid notes almost seeming to tap on the crystals of the chandeliers overhead until they sparkled slow, languid light across the dance floor.

Her gaze followed a particular flicker of light across the room until it shimmered at the base of someone's shiny black shoes.

Her heart beat erratically as her eyes followed the slim outline of the man's legs from where he sat in a large gold and red throne, up to his torso dressed in a silky black vest and a deep burgundy coat. A gold crown lined with red rubies adorned the top of his head. And when her gaze landed on the gold of his eyes...

Ellie's breath hitched.

King Rylan Rhapsody was a rather pretty sight to behold, and she wasn't the only one looking.

Whether obvious or not, nearly everyone in the room held their attention on the Mad King from where he lounged in his throne chair, gazing out over the throngs of people dressed in fancy suits and beautiful dresses. One after another, guests approached the bottom of the dais and bowed low. He hardly spared anyone a glance.

She nervously smoothed down the fabric of her skirt. What if he dismissed her so casually like all the others? It would be better if she hadn't come at all.

Yet, her feet refused to move as if her shoes found themselves glued to the floor. To willingly leave such a breathtaking ball would be a crime.

But it wouldn't be her first time committing a crime...

A group of ladies several paces away drew her attention, keeping her lingering in the shadows for just a while longer.

One of the ladies fixed the enormous flower in her hair as large as a hat, her voice a haughty tone filled with terrible offense. "It's about time he chooses a wife and produces an heir for the Wonderland throne, is it not?"

Another lady scoffed. "He has no interest in dabbling with women." She grinned and lowered her voice. "I've heard he's frightened of them. Runs away when they get too close."

The third woman rolled her eyes and snapped her fan closed. "He can't tinker with his roses for the rest of his life. If not him, someone must take the initiative."

The woman sauntered across the dance floor, couples moving out of her path and bowing as if she held a high status in society. She approached the dais, several steps separating herself from the king. Rylan didn't whatsoever lift his gaze to her. Rather, he rested his chin in his hand, looking bored as he stared not at the dancers but toward the window and the darkness raining down outside.

Clearing her throat, the woman dipped into a low curtsy. "Your Highness."

As if he hadn't heard her at all, he continued to stare out the window.

The woman's eye twitched as she rose from her curtsy. "Your Highness," she repeated. Nothing. And then she stepped forward, lifting a hand toward him. "Your Majes—"

Finally, Rylan lifted only two of his fingers, and the guards standing in front of him crossed their spears together to block the woman's advancement. "Do not touch me," he hissed vehemently. "Guards, throw her out of the castle!"

"But Your Majesty! Please forgive my offense. I meant no harm."

Despite her pleas, the Mad King waved a hand, and the guards complied by escorting her out of the ballroom and out of sight. Perhaps this was Ellie's cue to leave.

However, just as she took the first step toward her retreat, Piper Pixiewing appeared suddenly, grabbed her arm, and flitted her wings, pulling her along. "Come on!"

"Come on where?" Her first instinct was to dig her feet into the floor to slow herself.

"Wonderland tradition indicates you must present yourself to the king if he's seated. Otherwise, it's bad manners."

"Manners?" she squeaked. "I wasn't aware Wonderland had manners at all!"

Piper giggled and glanced over her shoulder to cast her a look of amusement. "You're silly. No wonder Rylan likes you!"

"No!" she gasped, digging her feet further until she swore the soles of her shoes started smoking. They didn't really, but somehow, they still felt hot beneath her feet. "I think I'd rather return to the apothecary. This really isn't my usual haunt."

Well, not like this at least.

Somehow, she managed to take back her wrist from the pixie, but when she turned around, she ran directly into Gideon Glimmer wearing an extra tall hat as long as her arm and a reflective monocle, likely for the stupendous occasion.

"Ah!" the man exclaimed with his arms outstretched. "I was just coming to escort you. Lend an old man your arm, hmm?"

Old man?

Ellie blinked slowly as she tried to find any indication that the man before her was old at all. His hair was free of gray, and no wrinkles lined the corners of his eyes. In fact, he might have looked even younger than Rylan if not for the monocle giving him a mature, sophisticated air.

"I was just leaving," she said with strangled laughter.

She tried to step around him, but he stepped to the side to block her path. "You can leave in a minute. I'm terribly embarrassed to greet the king without someone on my arm."

Without her realizing it, their arms were linked as they walked slowly out of the shadows and into the ballroom.

"You see," the man continued, "Rylan is always making fun of me for showing up empty handed to these types of events. Would you spare a poor man a little mockery?"

A sigh escaped her, pity deep in her soul for this supposedly old man who received the bitter end of Rylan's mockery. Who didn't?

"Fine. Lead the way."

However, the closer they approached the dais, the more her heart thrummed, and her fingers fretted. What would Rylan think? Would he mock her for her gown? Not even taking into consideration that he'd picked it out in the first place. Would he throw her out of the castle like he'd done to the last woman who had approached? What if he was now in a bad mood? She'd prefer to make herself scarce over publicly announcing herself to the ballroom at large.

As if sensing her anxiety, Gideon patted her hand and offered a reassuring smile.

They continued forward, the sea of guests parting for them and simultaneously staring with slack jaws or judging eyes. Not at her, though, surely. Rather, it was more likely they were gawking at Gideon's ridiculously tall hat and overly shiny monocle.

Finally, the crowd parted entirely, and she broke through the sea of guests to face Rylan directly.

His eyes flashed wide open the moment they landed on her, and he shot upright from his bored and slumped posture, his feet smacking the floor with a thud. His hand darted to his wrist where he proceeded to absently rub it back and forth like a nervous tick, the faintest bit of color climbing to his ears.

It seemed he was just as affected by Gideon's tall hat like the rest of them because it certainly wasn't her. No one had looked at her like that since Melgren. Even then, she knew his affections had been a hoax to freely get her to lend magical aid.

Gideon dipped into a bow. Ellie quickly scrambled to follow suit with an awkward bow which then turned into a curtsy halfway through in her sudden fluster. Now she wanted to hide entirely after the entire ballroom of guests and their dogs had witnessed her blunder.

A grin lifted on Rylan's mouth as he casually leaned to one side of his throne. "Red is my favorite color. Have I ever mentioned that?"

"At least once, sire," she replied, overly aware that the music lowered in volume, and many guests glued their gazes to them like sap trapping unfortunate insects within its embrace.

Her attention darted to the crown he wore atop his head, and for the strangest reason, her heart picked up its pace in her chest. This was still the annoying, headache-inducing Rylan she had known over the past several weeks. So why did her heart flutter about nervously like a butterfly skillfully evading a hunter's net?

"It looks even better on you than it did on Julian Jester."

A snort escaped her, and she quickly covered it with a cough behind her hand. "You're telling me you had your friend try it on first?"

"Of course, dear. He's about your height. I needed to make sure you wouldn't be tripping yourself silly."

"How considerate of you."

"I do try."

"Poor Julian."

Rylan waved a nonchalant hand. "The man adores fashion. It was hardly a burden for him. I think he might have been almost as excited as I to see you wear it."

With all her might, she tried to hold back the warmth wanting to fill her face. Rylan was full of insincere compliments. Now was no different.

Thankfully, Gideon took control of the conversation next. "Thank you for your hospitality, Your Highness. We will be sure to enjoy ourselves at the ball."

Ellie turned to leave, relief lending energy to the soles of her feet itching to run. But with a lift of his hand, Rylan halted them in their tracks and beckoned her forward. Not Gideon, but her.

Hesitantly, she approached, still wary of everyone watching her every movement. Rylan stood from this throne and met her halfway, standing two steps above her.

He held out a hand, and knowing his unpredictable temperament, she was hesitant to react. However, she also lifted her hand but kept it aloft over his. Close but not touching.

He bent at the waist and kissed the air above her fingers, eliciting a wide range of gasps around the room and an unforgiving blush in her own cheeks. Shock shimmied down her spine at the unexpected action. Of all the weird things Rylan had said or done, this rose somewhere to the top of the list.

She dropped her hand to her side and schooled her expression. She'd been caught up in a man's charms once, and although Rylan wasn't anywhere near as deceptive or sneaky as Melgren, he was still ingenuine.

She tried her best to ignore the way her hand warmed as if his kiss lingered on her fingers despite them not touching to begin with. Any warmer, and the glove she wore just might catch fire.

Without another word, she dipped into a curtsy and turned around, following the same path she'd previously walked. After a few moments, she glanced back at the throne...

...only to discover Rylan's absence. His seat sat empty as if he'd disappeared with the single snap of his fingers. As far as she knew, none of his dying roses held such power.

When dozens of eyes still followed her every movement, her discomfort won over any sliver of desire to stay a moment longer. She attempted to remain calm and unhurried as she crossed the ballroom, only wishing for a mask to hide the rising panic in her expression. There were too many people. Too many eyes. Too much music and light and guests. She wanted the dim atmosphere of the apothecary and the safety of books and herbs and potions.

But walls of people blocked her path, causing her lungs to suffocate more with each minute she remained trapped in the ballroom. When pushing her way out of the room failed, she ducked into the shadows against the wall, a hand to her heart as she attempted to catch her breath.

With a flick of her magic, she could have parted a sea of disgruntled ball guests, taking in the accompanying curses with amusement and snide mockery. But with her power locked…

She was at the mercy of the crowd.

As the panic grew within her, she glanced around helplessly for the same door she'd entered through. But with all the chaos around her, she'd gotten herself turned around and now found herself unable to locate a single way of escape.

Why had she come? This had been a mistake.

Just as she took a step forward in an attempt to brave the crowds once more, or even to ask one of the palace guards for directions, something hooked around her waist and yanked her backward.

Her cry of surprise was swallowed by a hidden door behind her and soft candlelight flickering shadows across the wall. She glanced at her waist to find herself hooked by a shepherd's cane. Indignation rose within her, and she quickly spun around to witness the mischievous smirk playing at the corners of the infuriating Mad King's mouth.

Torn between poking him hard in the eyeball and kicking his shin, she turned away instead, only to face a hidden door now closed like the dead end of a hallway. And she had no idea how to open it.

However…

Would she rather face the unyielding crowds of the ballroom? Or the headaches lying in wait for her the moment Rylan opened his mouth?

It was hard to say…

"Caught you, Your Sorceressness." His grin widened as he pulled her closer, hand over hand on the shepherd's cane until the hem of her dress nearly brushed against his boots. Nearly, of course. Because not in any timeframe would he touch even the smallest part of her on purpose.

Her indignation rose from her heart and into her eyes as a blazing glare. "And are you the sort to catch and release? Or to catch and flay?"

Rylan tapped his mouth with a single gloved finger. "I haven't decided yet. It's been a while since I've gone fishing, after all."

He walked backward, pulling her along by the cane until she truly felt like an animal led around by its master. She wanted to dig her heels into the lush carpet beneath her feet, to shy away from the sconces lighting their way down the hallway. But where would she go otherwise? Only Rylan knew where they were.

"I can follow you just fine on my own," she said with a huff, trying to push herself out of the crook of the cane but failing when he only increased his pace to keep the cane from going slack against her.

He only grinned at her over his shoulder. "But this is far more fun, no?"

The hallway opened into a spacious room with windows stretching from floor to ceiling. Moonlight shimmered through the glass, its glimmering sparkles caressing the translucent barrier like flakes of snow.

Beneath her feet lay smooth tiles reflecting the light from sconces flickering across the room and providing a soft, gentle light to the atmosphere around them. Beautiful. Soft. Delicate. She'd never experienced such a serene atmosphere.

"What is this place?" she asked breathlessly. "There's no one here."

Rylan's voice turned somber. "It was my mother's favorite room. She liked to view the stars within the comfort of a warm palace, and this room has a lot of windows. No one is allowed in here. It holds too many painful memories of my mother."

"Then why bring me here?"

He shrugged, his nonchalant grin returning to his face. "You two would have gotten along quite splendidly. I think she would have liked to meet you."

What kind of woman was Rylan's mother? If his father was anything like him, then surely, she must have dealt with a lot of headaches herself. Unless he'd taken more after his mother.

Before she pondered on it further, Rylan used the cane to spin her in a circle around him.

At first, she frowned, trying to struggle away. But then laughter came unbidden to her lips when she realized this was like dancing. She'd never danced before, only watched from afar. But this…this… Oh, it was delightful!

"We're dancing," she laughed, eyes blazing with amusement. "You could have just asked for a dance in the ballroom."

"And give my subjects more reason to mock me?" He pulled her close, then guided her back like the steps of a real dance. "Parading about the dance floor with a cane separating me from my partner would do wonders for my reputation."

"The upper world forbid you tarnish it any further by giving the ladies at court more kindling for their gossip."

"You understand! How fortunate."

He spun her again, and this time, she allowed the muffled music from far away and the shimmering moonlit atmosphere to drop her guard entirely. She closed her eyes and leaned back against the cane, her arms spread out on either side of her as she felt the rhythm and flow of the dance consume her soul in the most tantalizing way.

For so long, she'd chased after things she could never have. Yearning to dance with someone who cared for her, who might protect her and keep her safe, even if for a few moments.

With a start, she realized she hadn't thought of King Melgren in a long while. The more time she spent with Rylan, the more her heart healed.

Like now, as it burned several shades lighter within her chest.

She opened her eyes to find Rylan watching her as he spun her in slow circles around himself. Was she imagining the softness in his eyes? The tender way he seemed to look at her?

He dropped the cane to the ground, still leading her in a dance without a single brush of his hand. Nearly wrist to wrist. Almost shoulder to shoulder. Hands three slivers apart. She'd watched plenty of dancing in her past, and she'd never learned how to dance. But he led her expertly without even a single touch of his hand.

She hadn't realized they'd stopped dancing until Rylan spoke, pulling her out of the deep sea of gold in his eyes. "Would you stay here?" he asked quietly.

"Hmm?" Her thoughts were muddled by the deep rasp of his voice, by the bottomless emotion in his eyes.

"If I asked you to stay in Wonderland, would you?"

"Oh…I…" She pulled her hand away and took a step backward. "I'm not sure if I belong here. I have obligations…"

He grinned at her. "You can curse people here, too, you know. Everyone needs a hobby. Might be loads of fun."

Unable to help herself, she laughed. "I would be lying if I said that wasn't a tempting offer."

However, she didn't want to answer. Because confusing emotions ran rampant through her heart, and they wouldn't still long enough for her to make sense of the warmth and joy, the chill and fear. Something was very wrong. Her first instinct was to flee.

"Which is the way back to my room?" she asked.

Rylan twirled his finger in a circle in the air. "Pick a door and find out."

Internally, she sighed. It seemed the only options before her was either getting lost or finding herself with a raging headache. Saving herself the trouble, she walked across the room and chose a door at random. When she turned the handle, the door honked at her.

"Ah!" she cried, stumbling backward.

Behind her, Rylan laughed. "Not that door, probably. Try another one."

"Insolent child!" the door cried, a pair of blinking eyes suddenly showing within the wood. It wrinkled its doorknob nose. "At least ask permission first before twisting someone's snout."

More laughter from Rylan. It seemed she would be attaining that headache after all.

She rolled her eyes at him and tried another door. This time, it opened without protest. She almost stepped through but glanced over her shoulder to find Rylan's attention on her. "Thank you for the dance. I enjoyed myself tonight." She paused. "Are you returning to the ballroom?"

He turned his gaze toward the moonlight shining through the windows, a wistful look in his eyes. "I think I'll stay here for a little while longer."

The sight of his expression twisted her heart in the most strangely delightful way. She quickly stepped through the door and shut it behind her. And then she leaned against the wall with her eyes closed, holding a hand to her thrumming heart as her thoughts stilled, and she finally made sense of the emotions swirling inside her.

With a startling awareness…

She realized she was beginning to fall in love with King Rylan Rhapsody.

What an unfortunate turn of events.

15

Follow The White Rabbit

"It's done!" Ellie exclaimed, her hands resting on her hips as she stepped back to view her handiwork.

Rylan frowned, his eyebrows furrowed as he glanced at the white rabbit squirming within Thaddeus Thimble's arms. "What did you do, exactly?"

It looked like any normal rabbit. Just a bit squirmy and ready to bolt. True, he'd never had many dealings with rabbits, but he still doubted the furry thing would lead them to the correct destination.

Without warning, the ground beneath them trembled, causing him to lose his balance and stumble forward. Gideon Glimmer rushed forward as if to catch him, but then seeming to remember the no touching rule, he lifted his hands in the air and evaded.

Rylan crashed to the ground, receiving a face full of turf and a fatigued body gasping for energy like a man dying of thirst. He spat out several blades of grass and glared at his friend.

"You could have at least pretended to miss," Rylan grumbled.

Gideon offered a guilty smile while fixing his monocle. "Then you'd have found another reason to complain."

Next to him, Ellie snorted but quickly covered the sound with her hand. He shot her a glare and dusted himself off as he once more found his feet. He opened his mouth to retort, but the ground began shaking again. *Thump, thump, thump.*

The Wonderland giant sprinted behind the mountain's horizon with the sun beneath its arm, a triumphant grin on its face at its new catch. The sunlight dispersed the darkness, giving way to a very sudden sunset and chasing away all the beautiful moonbeams of the past several weeks. But then the giant tripped, and a vibrating *thud* shook the earth for a few moments, followed by silence.

The giant did not get up again. But the sun lingered just below the mountaintops, splashing glorious orange, yellow, and pink colors across the sky.

"Uh…" Ellie stared after the fallen giant. "Will he be alright?"

Rylan waved a hand. "He's fine, he's fine. He'll likely sleep for a while after that fall, though."

Ellie shook her hand and pinched the bridge of her nose. "Wonderland is the strangest realm I've ever encountered."

"Out of two, right?"

Right on time, the sorceress rolled her eyes. Ha! Getting under her skin was too easy and fun.

"You'd better leave quickly," Gideon said as he led two horses by the reins and approached Rylan and Ellie "The white rabbit will sooner scratch up Thaddeus's face than allow him to hold it for another minute."

Piper, Cleo, and Luna pulled Ellie into a fierce embrace. Sparkling, unshed tears lined Piper's eyes. "In case we don't see you for a while! But you must promise to return. Promise us!"

"I will," Ellie promised.

Rylan turned his shoulder to hide the faint smile tugging on his lips. Whatever happened after this… At least he could count on the sorceress coming back if she honored her word. Because…he kinda…liked her. Just a little bit. She was entertaining at the very least. And their friendship was interesting. He thought he might actually miss her if she left Wonderland.

"Good luck." Gideon patted his shoulder, a worried look in his eyes. If Rylan failed this task… Wonderland was doomed. He wasn't entirely sure what Alice's plan was, but it couldn't be good.

He glanced from Gideon to Thaddus to Felix before his attention landed on the women. He wouldn't fail. Whatever it took, he promised himself to see this through, whatever the cost.

He mounted his horse, taking control of the reins just as Ellie mounted hers. He said to his friends, "Take care of Wonderland in my absence. I'll try not to be gone long."

And with that, Thaddeus released the white rabbit. The creature sprinted down the path, and he kicked his horse in a quick canter to follow with Ellie's horse thundering behind.

This would work. It *had* to work.

After what felt like an hour, his eyes hurt from straining to follow the rabbit through winding forest paths and around thickets of bushes. He and Ellie traded places, and they followed at a slower pace when the rabbit continued forward more leisurely. Ellie assured him that the rabbit hadn't lost the scent, but the slower progress spurred a burst of anxiety in his chest.

Another hour passed, and he struggled not to nod off in his saddle. He closed his eyes for only a few moments before Ellie started cursing. Rylan's eyes snapped wide open, and he kicked his horse forward to walk side by side with her. "What happened?"

"What do you mean, what happened? I got cursed! Again!" She pulled back her sleeve and shoved her wrist beneath his nose. "What even is this?"

His eyes widened as shock coursed through his body, trembling to his innermost core. Like the black spade on his wrist, she sported a red heart on hers, unmistakable like the purest drop of blood shaped perfectly on her skin.

He pinched the bridge of his nose and exhaled a long and slow breath. Of course, he'd suspected... But to have his suspicions confirmed without room for doubt?

Ellie truly was his fated person. And even worse... He didn't even *need* the mark to confirm it. Perhaps he'd known since the first moment they'd made eye contact. Something had sparked between them, and it continued to burn with each passing day.

But instead of confirming what he knew out loud...

He wore his best puzzled frown and stroked his chin. "How odd. It must indeed be quite the curse. Such misfortune."

"Do you know what kind of curse it is?"

He turned a shoulder to her to keep from laughing. "I might. But our deal didn't include a clumsy fortune telling, now, did it?" His shoulders started shaking as he tried his best to hold back his amusement. He very much enjoyed teasing her, even better when she released an exasperated huff.

To take his teasing one step further…

"I may be willing to make a trade."

Her eyes looked ready to roll at any moment. How delightful! "What type of trade?"

A smirk lifted on his lips, and her gaze followed its upward movement. Now her eyes appeared *extremely* ready to roll. "The information you want in exchange for a kiss. I've been told I'm a good kisser."

"By whom?" she laughed. Although her eyes didn't roll, he'd still managed to elicit laughter from her. "You've been avoiding women for most of your life."

He winked and pulled out his pocket watch. "By you in about twenty seconds."

She rolled her eyes. And there it was. A point for him! "Nice try. That sort of charm doesn't work on me."

He snapped his fingers dejectedly. "Can't blame a madman for trying."

They continued forward with a smile on each of their faces, the atmosphere much lighter than it had been only minutes prior. With a foreboding destination in front of them, they needed to hold onto every sliver of light available until they couldn't anymore.

As the hours passed, they took turns leading so the other could take a break from the constant eye strain from watching the rabbit dart back and forth between bushes. They didn't dare stop for even a moment, afraid even the shortest rest would make them lose their target.

"Soooo…" Rylan said to diffuse the unwelcoming silence of the forest. "You know my favorite color. What's yours?"

She lifted an eyebrow. "Truly? What childish nonsense."

"Ah!" He held a hand over his face and turned away. "Must you always wound me? Mentioning my age in comparison to yours?" He peeked between his fingers to find her grinning. She spurred her horse faster to catch up with him before playfully kicking his stirrup without touching him.

"Green. Like the forests back home."

He now stared at her straight posture where she expertly sat in the saddle. "And how do Wonderland's forests compare?"

"Aside from the terrifying creatures lurking in every shadow?" She grinned again. "They're fine, I suppose."

Ahead of them, the rabbit stopped suddenly and lowered its ears, instantly putting him on high alert. With agile movements, he jumped quietly to the ground and crept forward, wary of the shouts and clinking metal ahead.

He peeked around the corner of a tree, only for his blood to freeze in his veins.

Up ahead lay a towering gray fortress crawling with numerous guards. How were they ever going to get in now?

16
A Rhyme a Day Keeps the Anxiety Away

Ellie gawked at the fortress towering from one end of the forest to the other. White and blue flags flapped in the wind with the head of a lion emblazoned in gold in the middle. Guards dressed in metal armor and blue capes roamed about the parapet and in front of the gates.

Exactly who was this Alice person? Because she wasn't the normal girl Rylan had explained her to be.

She anxiously rubbed her thumb over her palm as she watched as groups of people wearing fine dresses and suits were stopped by the guards and questioned before being allowed inside. A long line of carriages drew up one by one, pulled by strange creatures that looked like horses but were more skeletal with a burning blue fire visible in their core.

At this point, the creatures of Wonderland shouldn't surprise her. But it came as a shock, nonetheless.

"I think we should have broken my curse first before attempting this," Ellie lamented, pinching the bridge of her nose. "At least I'd have my magic."

"Wonderland would collapse before we managed to make it back."

"And it still might at this point. There are a hundred guards and only two of us. Why didn't you bring your soldiers with us?"

"Because," Rylan drawled with a flip of his hand. "If Alice noticed an entire battalion headed her way, she'd simply crush my heart and doom Wonderland. The less people who attempt this, the higher the success we might face." His expression contorted into a grimace. "Face. Lace. Grace. Mace. Chase. Pace. Race."

"Stop rhyming!" she hissed.

"I can't!" He wiped his palms on his trousers. "I rhyme when I get nervous."

"I thought you rhymed because it was a good exercise for the mind?"

"Of course not!" he spluttered, a flush crawling from his cheeks to his ears. "I also lie when I get a little flustered. Are you going to hold it against me?"

Her mouth fell agape as she stared at him. "Yes! No more lying, Rylan!"

He closed his eyes and hissed pleasantly through his teeth, touching his thumb and pointer finger together. "I do enjoy when you yell at me. How irresistible!"

"I'm serious!"

"Fine! Just because you asked somewhat nicely, I'll stop lying. Happy?"

"I'd be happier if we weren't in this position in the first place."

He scowled. "Would you like me to go in by myself? You've gotten me this far. I suppose I can't ask for more."

Ellie pinched the bridge of her nose harder. The offer was tempting. But...

She glanced sideways at him, at the way a strand of black hair flipped perfectly over his golden eyes, at his chiseled jaw and pert mouth. Her heart picked up within her, a prickling sensation crawling from shoulder to shoulder as her heart transitioned into several shades lighter. No longer was a black heart beating within her chest, but one resembling the first blossoms of a new love.

Instinct warned her to fight against it, especially considering what happened the last time she'd fallen in love. But another part of her wanted to embrace it, to fall backward into its warm waters and bask in the sunshine glow.

What am I thinking? she chided herself as she pinched her arm to pull herself out of the unrealistic imaginings. She'd learned from the last time that love was not a feeling to trifle with. All it brought was doom and misery. This instance was no different.

"I'm not about to abandon you now," she said quietly.

They surreptitiously moved off the path and deeper into the trees to conceal themselves from watchful eyes. When they were out of earshot and out of view, Rylan turned to her, a serious note in his eyes.

"Do you sense any traps ahead?"

Without her magic, she couldn't *sense* the traps, per say. But she hadn't lived for over two centuries not to notice the workings of one.

She nodded. "The walls have traps galore. Probably to prevent a nosy king from clambering over the parapet."

Rylan grinned, twirling a lock of hair around his finger. "You think I'm nosy? What a high compliment!"

"If I could shove you, I would."

"I dare you to try. I have a lot of good punishments up my sleeve waiting to be used."

She ignored him, though she found it incredibly difficult when his scent alone filled every breath she took. "Back to the issue at hand. There are traps on the walls and a barrier preventing anyone from entering the fortress without permission. If we're to succeed at getting in, we must go through the front door."

"Looking like this? I don't think so. I'm highly conspicuous. Hmm… It must be the crown."

"I don't think it's just the crown." Everything about him exuded the presence of important royalty. Even the color of his eyes. A sigh escaped her. "You should have brought some roses."

"Who said I didn't?"

He dug a hand down the front of his tunic and pulled out a dome-shaped pendant covered with frosty green glass. He dangled the pendant in front of her face. "It's a portable greenhouse! Do you like it?"

"I…uh…" She leaned forward to inspect it, but just as quickly, Rylan snatched it back.

"Now who's the nosy one, hmm?" He shook out the chain as if snapping open a dirty rug. The small greenhouse grew larger in front of them. Rylan set it on his lap, unlatched the little door, and stuck his hand inside. His tongue pressed against the side of his mouth as if deep in thought before he stuck his entire arm inside the door.

She craned her neck to glance at the other side of the greenhouse, only to find frosted green glass with no hand in sight. What was this magic? And how could she emulate such a feat back home? It would be a handy little instrument for her herbs during the chilly winter season.

Finally, Rylan pulled out a beautifully preserved purple rose with blossoming petals completely unlike the ones wilting in his garden. It was as if the flower was untouched by time and misfortune.

At least until she noticed the edges of the rose beginning to wilt inward. Out of the greenhouse, it wasn't likely to survive without the Heart of Wonderland.

"Alright, here's the plan," Rylan said, unfazed by the slow wilt of the flower in his hand. "We must be quick, but this should work." He pricked his finger on one of the thorns on the stem, a droplet of blood trailing to his palm. "Purple is for shapeshifting. Since they will likely recognize my face, I need you to give this rose to someone and have them prick their finger on it. Only then can I shapeshift into the person pricked. Alice has never seen your face before. We can use that to our advantage."

She nodded, fascinated by the dark magic involved in such a feat. Rylan was incredibly powerful. It always astounded her to learn what things he could accomplish with his roses.

"And who should I prick?"

He drummed his fingers on his knees. "One of the guests. That way we can get inside without too much scrutiny." He wrinkled his nose as if overcome by an obstacle. "Oh, bleary dreary."

"What is it?"

"If there are two guests with the same face showing up at the gates, it will cause issues and tip Alice off. How good are you at knocking someone out?"

"Rylan!"

"What? It's necessary for the good of the kingdom!"

Oh, bleary dreary, indeed. A headache was starting to come on. "I've brought a few herbs with me. The sap from one should be potent enough to knock someone out if inhaled. I'm sure I can figure it out."

"Good, good." He offered the rose to her, but just as she reached for it, he held it aloft. "It's incredibly important to do this correctly. Place your fingers directly beneath the flower so you don't prick yourself."

She rolled her eyes. Treating her like a clumsy child. The nerve! She reached out again to take the flower from him. "I know how to hold a rose, Rylan," she scoffed. But then something sharp stabbed her finger. "Ow!"

They stared back at each other with bewildered expressions.

He hissed between his teeth and shook his head. "That was my last one." He clapped his hands. "New plan! I take on your image, and we present ourselves as twins. How well can you dance?"

"I'm not letting you become me! That's just...just... I don't know. Odd!"

He huffed. "You see? This is why I don't tell others about my magic. It unsettles people."

"Really?" she asked sarcastically.

"Don't worry overly much. I'll become the male version of you. Is that better?"

"No?"

"Well, we're all out of roses—and options—darling. What else do you suggest?"

She scowled at him as she dug into the saddle bags on the horse and shoved a pair of clothes into his arms. "Just do what you have to do."

Alice Full of Malice

Ellie wasn't fully prepared to find herself staring back at an almost mirror image of herself, except the other person had short hair, a wider jaw, and stood a few inches taller.

Rylan grinned as he turned in a full circle, showing off his sleeveless vest, which dipped down to reveal a small portion of a smooth chest. The pants he wore matched the color of her green skirt, the boots a similar brown to her rope sash. Aside from the gender differences, they were identical in every other way.

"Unnerving…" she commented, reaching out to touch his face. But he ducked beneath her hand and glared at her.

"I may look fabulous, but still no touching."

"You look just like me…" She lifted a hand again, unable to help herself. He leaped backward and ducked behind a tree, placing the trunk between them. He peeked out only to double down on his glare.

"I mean it," he warned. "All this effort will be useless if one of us—when I say one of us, I absolutely mean you—are face down dead in the dirt! No touching!"

A snicker escaped her mouth, but she abandoned her efforts in favor of a twirl of her own. She looked the part of a dancer. But they both very well knew she hardly knew how to dance. At the very least, the disguise might get them inside the fortress. She couldn't promise anything more.

"Ready?" she asked.

"No. Let's go."

With trepidation rising within her heart, they secured their mounts to nearby trees and slipped into a large group approaching the fortress with wagons and horses and colorful banners. As they neared the fortress, her hands became slick with anxiety. She came up with several different escape plans in her mind if this went sideways.

As they moved closer, she eyed the hidden traps on the walls and the guards staring down at arriving guests from the parapet. Alice was somewhere within these fortress walls. What would they do if they happened to run into her before finding Rylan's heart?

She glanced sideways at him. If they didn't reunite him with the Heart of Wonderland, he'd likely die within the next few days or so. He wouldn't be able to hold on much longer.

When the group in front of them was allowed into the fortress, she and Rylan attempted to follow closely behind.

"Halt!" One of the guards tipped his spear to the side to block their entrance. "State your name and purpose."

Rylan waved a flamboyant hand. "We're Tweedle Dee—"

"—and Tweedle Dum!" Ellie quickly finished for him, worried he might give away their disguise with his voice alone. It was distinctive. Along with his flamboyant air, it wouldn't be impossible to be discovered despite looking like her male twin. "We're traveling—"

"—performers, at your service! Our troupe just went through, and they'd surely be put out should they have to skip our performance."

Oh, she wanted to strangle him! She cast him a brief warning glare to shut up, but he only grinned.

"Entertainers, eh?" the guard asked, lifting a brow. "Well, then. Let's see it. Give me a good show."

Ellie resisted smacking herself in the forehead. What other talents did Rylan possess other than giving people headaches and ridiculous punishments for silly crimes? Of course, the man could dance. He could dance very well, in fact. But showing off his ballroom feet might land them in the mud of suspicion. They really should have figured out all these details before approaching the fortress.

Rylan patted his pockets, turning in a full circle as if searching for something. "Ah!" He lifted a finger, his eyes lighting up, before reaching into his breast pocket and pulling out a bubble wand made of pliable wood.

By now, a small group crowded around them. Ellie wished to shoo them away to avoid drawing further notice, but at this point, it might only cause more harm than good.

She watched with bated breath as Rylan turned the bubble wand upside down and repeatedly dipped it in the air in front of him. She was just as surprised as their audience when he lifted the wand to his mouth and blew out a bubble! But it wasn't just any ordinary bubble. It looked like it was filled with water, floating through the air inches over his hand.

Soon, two other bubbles joined the first, and Rylan began juggling them in the air. What type of magical device was this bubble wand? She'd never seen anything like it, nor had she known he'd kept it on his person for however long.

"Tweedle Dum, catch!" Rylan tossed one of the water orbs to her, but she lifted her hands too slowly to make the catch. Rather than bouncing off her like a bubble might do, the entire thing popped and splashed over her head, soaking her in a bucket's worth of water.

She gasped at the sudden chill dripping from her hair and down her back. But they were performers. It was supposed to be part of the act. Therefore, when Rylan dropped the other two orbs to the ground in what appeared to be momentary shock, she lifted her hands and curtsied in a "Ta-da!" type of gesture. The Mad King followed suit with an overexaggerated bow.

The guard laughed and lifted his spear to allow them entrance. "Idiots. Go on through."

They walked side by side through the gates and into the fortress. When a stone awning cast shadows over them, she leaned closer to Rylan. "You are despicable!" she hissed near his ear, water still dripping from her chin.

"Have I told you that I love when you're angry with me?" He grinned, the faintest hint of guilt in his eyes.

She barely resisted stomping on his foot. Ridiculous king. She hated that she loved his teasing and his banter and his unpredictability. Everything about him went against her nature as a sorceress. She shouldn't like him.

Yet, she did.

He was charming in the most maddening way.

They followed the rest of the guests through another set of doors, down a long corridor, and into a room that opened into a spacious area. Long blue banners draped from towering ceilings. Guards lined every wall like stiff displays of suits and armor. And sitting on a throne at the front of the room…

A woman with blonde hair draping down her back wore a blue dress with white frills on the hems of the sleeves and skirt. Painted on either temple was the shape of a red diamond, while a black heart rested between her brows. She stared out over the crowd as if looking for something. Or perhaps…*someone.*

Rylan inhaled sharply as he slipped behind a large group of half-giants to conceal himself. She followed suit.

"Tweedle Dum!" he hissed. "Any brilliant plans now?"

"Don't call me that!" she hissed back.

"You named yourself! You can't blame me. Besides…I think it suits you."

He snickered behind his hand. Despite his outward levity, she noticed the way his pupils contracted with fear and how his hands shook if he kept them still long enough. He must have been terrified of Alice after what she'd done to him.

Ignoring his jibe for his sake, she nodded her head and took a step closer. "Without my magic, I can't be sure how accurate this will be. But we can try."

Glancing back and forth across the room to make sure no one watched her movements, especially not Alice, she extracted a needle from a small pouch attached to her belt and gestured for Rylan to hold out his arm.

He squeezed his eyes shut and turned his head away but offered his finger anyway. She rolled her eyes. Was this really the man who often pricked his fingers on his roses to evoke his magic? How could he possibly run scared from her needle now?

When his fingers were covered by gloves, she instead pricked his lower arm, careful not to touch him, drawing just enough blood to coat the tip of the needle. Next, she slipped the needle into a vial filled with clear extract she'd prepared ahead of time, shaking it up to mix everything properly.

Over the din of the room, she instructed, "Now think of a happy memory embedded deep in your heart. It should evoke the spell."

After a few moments, a faint pink wisp gathered at the base of the vial and traveled through the room, down a lone corridor, and into the darkness of the unknown. She and Rylan should be the only ones able to see it, but just in case, they needed to hurry.

"Your heart is here," Ellie murmured. "Let's get going."

Following Rylan's lead, they snuck across the room, trying to avoid notice, and slipped into the dark corridor likely only used by servants judging by the fact that it was absent of guards. The quicker they found the heart and left this place behind, the better.

However, the two of them slowed when a voice grew louder behind them.

"Tonight marks a momentous occasion!" Alice said jubilantly, her voice echoing through the other room and into the corridor they traveled down. "It's the night of King Rhapsody's downfall!"

Cheers accompanied the woman's words, followed by excited chanting.

Alice continued, "No longer will we suffer under that tyrant's reign!"

More cheers.

Rylan shoved imaginary sleeves up to his elbows and turned around, but Ellie quickly stepped in his path. "Don't mind her words. Focus, King Rhapsody."

His attention pulled back to her as he scoffed. "That's Rylan to you! Don't you know how to address the King of Hearts properly?"

Headache... Headache! It pounded in her skull, forcing her to look to the ceiling as she took a deep, steadying breath. When she returned to the upper world, she planned to look into creating a medicine to help with headaches. Especially of the King of Hearts variety.

"Let's just go. We need to be quick about this."

They continued at a faster pace as they followed the wisp of pink strands leading through empty, dusty hallways and vacant rooms filled with old weapons or musty books. But one thing missing was people.

Soldiers... Servants... Guests... They were all missing, causing a growing pit of anxiety to rise within her. Either everyone was occupied, hence the empty corridors. Or something sinister waited for them up ahead.

Something scampered across her path. She stifled a scream and jumped to the side. Rylan twisted out of the way, narrowly avoiding them clashing together.

"Relax," he murmured. "It's just a mouse."

"Just a mouse? Like a regular mouse? Or one that opens its jaws super wide and swallows a person whole?"

Even in the darkness, she noticed the gleam of white teeth as he grinned. "The second one, obviously. This is Wonderland, darling."

He snickered and continued forward, leaving her entirely baffled. Was it really a creature that could swallow someone whole?

She shuddered and rushed to catch up to him, following only a step behind.

The pink wisps led them to a small, circular alcove at the end of the hallway, each wall crafted of rough stone bricks. When the pink wisps plummeted sharply downward and disappeared into the floor, they both sighed in frustration. Did they need to find a set of stairs to a lower floor? Why hadn't the wisps led them to a staircase to begin with?

"I don't like the look of this," she murmured, running a hand along the coarse stone walls. "A dead end is never a good sign."

"Unless you're stuck there with a beautiful woman." Rylan winked.

Ellie wanted to smack him, especially as his words fluttered her heart in the most aggravating way. He was too careless with his words, throwing them about like showering rain but meaning nothing he said.

"Look at this." She waved him over to show him a large fissure against the wall and floor, a whistle of wind flitting through the crack. "Something's down there."

"Perhaps our elusive staircase?"

Pushing herself to her feet, she planted her hands on her hips as she surveyed her surroundings. If a staircase lay beneath them, then there must be some sort of mechanism to unveil it.

She pushed away her frustration. With her magic, she'd be able to find it in an instant. Now it was up to guesswork.

They split up sides with her taking the left half of the circle and him the right. She brushed her fingers along the cracks and grooves in the wall and pulled on the empty sconces. Just when the thought occurred to give up and look elsewhere, something clicked behind her.

She only managed to turn her head to look over her shoulder before the entire floor disappeared beneath her feet.

A high-pitched scream erupted from her mouth—or perhaps it was from Rylan's—as they plummeted downward. Wind whipped through her hair. Something sharp stabbed her in the darkness, but she was so preoccupied with not dying that she flailed her arms and legs to grab onto something, anything at all, to break her fall.

Something stringy like vines slowed her descent, snapping with each violent twist and turn of her body, until finally, she landed on the ground in a heap.

A groan escaped her mouth, her body aching as she lifted her head to take in her surroundings. More stone walls surrounded them, the pink wisps leading them down yet another corridor.

"I'm weary of your traps!" Rylan shouted to the ceiling far above them as he leaped to his feet and kicked the wall. "They're no fun, anyway!"

Ellie pushed herself to a sitting position but inhaled sharply at the stabbing pain on her lower left abdomen. Ugh. She'd been injured in the fall.

Not only did her side hurt, but her ankle flared with pain as if she'd sprained it on her way down or from the rough landing. It didn't matter. They needed to continue forward.

"We have to keep looking," Ellie grunted, holding her side. "It has to be here. The pink wisps couldn't be wrong."

Rylan paced back and forth, back and forth, a distressed frown on his currently androgynous face. "I should have come more prepared. I should have anticipated Alice expecting me to come, to lure me into this maze full of traps and pointy objects. Why am I so foolish? I walked straight into her trap. What to do? What to do?"

Something warm trickled from the corner of Ellie's mouth. She quickly wiped it away with her sleeve to hide it from Rylan. "We keep going forward. I'm not sure we have any other choice."

"I should have left you behind. I should have…" He trailed off as he dug his fingers through his hair, the distraught look in his eyes increasing.

She forced a smile to her lips all while swallowing the metallic taste in her mouth. "This only means you have to stick it out with me to the end of my journey as well."

"Was that even a question?" he scoffed. "I don't care one whit about your quest, but I'm curious about the upper world and what it's like." Although he turned his back to her, she noticed him glancing at her from the corner of his eye. Perhaps he cared just a little bit.

He started forward, motioning for her to follow.

With great effort, she struggled to push herself to her feet. But the warmth in her abdomen only spread farther across her blouse, now too large for her hand to conceal. Dizziness spun her surroundings in circles. She coughed up another mouthful of blood, no longer able to tell which direction was the ceiling and which the floor.

She stumbled on her twisted ankle, losing her balance entirely, until she crashed onto the ground.

"Ellie!" Rylan cried, rushing toward her. He snatched a rotting plank of wood from where it rested against the wall and used it to turn her over onto her back. Through her spinning vision, she noticed the look of horror on his face as his gaze jumped from her mouth to her bleeding abdomen.

"Ellie," he choked, slumping to his knees beside her. "You're hurt."

"I-I-I'm fine," she spluttered through a mouthful of blood.

"No, you're not." His words escaped as a raspy croak. "This is my fault. I'm so sorry, Ellie. I'm so very sorry. Sorry. Mari. Chary. Starry."

Despite the situation, she managed a lazy grin. "I wasn't aware the King of Hearts was capable of apologizing. We'll mark the calendars for this momentous occasion. The people must celebrate the new holiday once a year."

"You think you're so funny. Well, you're not! Shrill-shrieking sorceress."

"Moody manipulative madman," she shot back.

She coughed again, her vision spinning so badly that she needed to shut her eyes to block out her disorienting surroundings. "K-k-keep going," she encouraged. "I'll still be here when you get back."

Rylan snorted. "Look at the sorry state of you. There will be nothing alive for me to return to."

Peeking her eyes open a crack, she watched as he dug into his vest and pulled out the miniature greenhouse pendant. It grew large enough to fit his arm, but this time, he pulled out a rose blooming with green petals.

"I thought you said you had no more roses."

Another snort as he pulled off only one of his gloves. "I said I had no more *purple* roses. I never said anything about green." Quieter, he said, "I never use these. Never had an occasion. But I do now."

Shock jolted through her as he pressed the thorny stem of the rose into her hand, their palms and fingers touching, enough to overpower the sting of the sharp thorns pricking her skin.

They…were touching. Skin to skin. Fingers to fingers. Palm to palm. With a single rose trapped between them. Not once had he ever touched her like this. On purpose. So why here? Why now?

"Rylan…" she murmured, a question in her voice.

"Shh. Just…quiet. Alright?"

"Alright," she whispered. And she let him hold her hand, the dark brown of his disguised eyes gazing down at her earnestly. The uncomfortable warmth from her abdomen traveled into her chest instead as she fully surrendered her heart and her trust to him. No longer was her heart marred black, but it pulsed a beautiful pink in color within her chest.

Never had she thought it possible to overcome her decades' worth of hatred and resentment. But here and now? All of it had evaporated into something lovely, something beautiful, something so foreign and long forgotten.

Although some of the pain lingered in her abdomen and her foot, it was mostly gone, healed by the flower.

"What did you do?" she asked.

He tossed the rose aside, now withered and crumbling to pieces upon impact with the ground. "Black roses siphon energy from other people and into me. Green siphons energy from me into other people."

"Rylan!" she gasped, shooting upright into a sitting position. But the remainder of the pain in her abdomen stopped her, and she grunted at the burning sensation still lingering there. "You hardly have enough energy as it is. You cannot give me any of what's left."

"Too late. It's already done."

Dark shadows lingered beneath his eyes. His face was paler than ever before. He looked closer to collapsing than making it out of this unscathed. But still, he stooped down, grabbed her arm, and hauled her upright until she rested across his shoulder with feet dangling off the ground.

"Put me down."

"I won't leave you behind."

"You have to."

"I won't!" His raised voice reverberated across the stone walls surrounding them. "I'll take the risk of touching you. But you're coming with me."

She wanted to weep. No one had ever treated her like this. Like she mattered. Like she was important. No one had ever chosen to stay by her side. But right here and now, Rylan did. He was braving his worst fear just to make sure she didn't get left behind.

The mustiness of the hallway quickly closed in on them, making it more difficult to breathe with each step. To distract them, she asked, "What happened, Rylan? To make you so afraid of your magic?"

A long silence stretched between them to the point where she thought he might not answer at all. She was about to ask a different question and change the subject when he finally spoke.

"I told you before that I grew up an orphan for most of my childhood." When she nodded against his shoulder, he continued, "My father died because of his own arrogance during a duel. But my mother…" He took a deep breath and let it out. She felt him trembling beneath her. "Just imagine what an ignorant child could do with the power of black roses but with his hands instead."

Ellie squeezed her eyes shut, her heart aching for that poor little boy who had lost his mother due to an unfortunate accident. At his own hands, no less! No wonder he'd feared touching another person. The death of his mother still haunted him.

That's when she realized…

Not too long ago, she'd suggested to Rylan to teach him how to control his power so he wouldn't have to fear touching others anymore. But now… It seemed he didn't even know that he'd perfected control through the use of his roses. To siphon only a little energy from others versus taking their life was far more mastery than she'd previously realized.

She surmised he wasn't likely to hurt her through his touch. But would he believe her?

"The wisps are slowing," Rylan commented before giving her a chance to respond to his confession.

They entered another circular room similar to the last, but rather than the wisps diving into the floor, they circled around a stone slab altar in the middle of the room…

…and the person sitting cross-legged on top, holding a pulsing pink crystal heart in her hand.

Alice.

Rylan's grip tightened around Ellie's arm as he froze in place, the two staring back at each other. Tension was strung tight in the air like the strings of an instrument ready to snap with the next thrum.

Alice grinned, bouncing her crossed leg up and down, up and down, where she sat. "How long have I known you, Rylan? You think a simple disguise is going to fool me?"

"You think this is a disguise?" Rylan replied flamboyantly, but Ellie caught the underlying anger coloring his words. "I enjoy parading around a new face now and again. It's fun."

"Ha. Of course, you do." Alice's attention shifted to the heart in her hand as she turned it around in a full circle. Dazzling pink light flickered across the wall, pulsing with unbelievable power. To think Ellie had once wanted this heart to give her the power to curse King Melgren. Objectively, it would have been an absolute waste when the power within could destroy mountains in the wrong hands. The weight of such a responsibility... No wonder Rylan was in a panic to get it back.

Gently, Rylan set her down on her feet but stood protectively in front of her. "Why didn't you destroy it before now?"

"Oh, I tried," Alice replied. "Many times. It's more resilient than I thought. Of course, that was *after* I attempted to use it for myself."

"And how did that work out for you?"

Without knowing the context between their conversation, even Ellie could guess what had happened. Such a powerful heart was likely to come with equally powerful protections. The only person who could use or destroy it was someone of royal Wonderland blood.

It was only a conjecture, but she'd studied magic long enough to understand its nuances.

In a flash of movement, Alice disappeared from the altar and reappeared behind Ellie before she even managed to blink. Cold metal pressed against her throat, and after releasing a shaky breath, she glanced down to find a dagger at her neck. Close to her skin but not touching.

"Stop. Stop!" Rylan raised a cautioning hand and took a step forward. But when Alice shifted the knife closer so the sharp point now touched Ellie's skin, he stopped in his tracks. "What do you want?"

This was all happening too fast. Ellie felt as if they'd only just arrived, but so many things had already gone wrong. Alice was smart. She'd known they would come.

"Release the enchantments on the heart."

"Don't do it, Rylan!" Ellie cried, but then she gasped when the blade nicked her neck. She needed to speak her peace, anyway, despite the danger to her life. "There are only two ways this will end, and neither are good for you."

"And you think I can just sit and watch you die? Ugh," he scoffed. "Sorceresses."

"Who would have thought?" Alice laughed near Ellie's ear. "You actually care for her. I thought I'd never see the day when you cared for anything other than yourself." She tipped her head to the side. "I'll skip the monologue about dethroning evil tyrants.

If you won't reverse the enchantments, then I have no further use for this woman."

Alice shifted her arm as if about to drag the blade across Ellie's throat, but Rylan threw up another cautioning hand.

"I'll do it!" he shouted. "I'll do it! Just release her."

Although Alice didn't release her, her grip slackened on her weapon, which allowed Ellie to take more than just a sip of breath. The other woman held out the heart, and Rylan approached.

"Use some sense here!" Ellie shouted. In the space of the past several weeks, she'd come to adore Wonderland's charms and the man who reigned over the strange land. Both were doomed if Rylan let Alice have her way.

Injured and weak without her magic, she was no match for Alice. But Rylan still had his magic. Surely, there was something he could still do.

"Sense is for the sane," Rylan said with a flip of his hand. Before she could call out for him to stop, he placed his hand on top of the heart.

A faint blast of power shot out from the heart in an array of pink and red light before fizzling like bubbles until the wisps disappeared, leaving behind a pulsing light. The protection enchantments had been lifted. Rylan was in danger.

Ellie leaped forward to try to snatch the heart out of the woman's fingers, but then a cold, icy chill burned through her chest, making it suddenly difficult to breathe.

Her eyes widened as she glanced down, only to find her own crystal pink heart pulsing in Alice's opposite hand dressed in a fingerless, metallic glove. Such was the chill of the shock that she was unable to move, unable to think clearly. How... Why...

"It seems..." Alice said with a smirk. "That your leverage is no longer needed."

And with the crush of her hand, she pulverized Ellie's heart into a thousand flakes of crystal before they scattered across the ground.

18

All Hail the Queen of Spades

Ellie collapsed to the ground, each breath raspy and labored without her heart to keep her alive. Rylan's body wanted to collapse with her in absolute devastation, but he knew that if he did nothing, she would not survive.

And perhaps…

Neither would he.

The sparks of Rylan's anger flew into a rage. He tore off his gloves, both hands bare for the first time in a very long time. It was as if his surroundings moved in a slow blur as Alice lifted the Heart of Wonderland in her palm, the malicious grin on her face betraying what she planned to do with it.

He moved faster than he ever thought possible as he rushed toward her, taking her by surprise. Alice's eyes widened only moments before he slammed his bare hand against her, directly over her own heart.

The magic and power he'd suppressed through his roses and lack of touch surged forth, jolting through his opponent. She threw her head back and screamed, her body convulsing where she stood before she slowly sank to her knees, and then her side, until she lay trembling on the ground. Rylan caught the Heart of Wonderland before it crashed to the ground, cradling it tenderly in his hands.

A soft red light pulsed through the crystal, calling him. Beckoning him. Enticing him. This was his. It belonged to him. With it, he could reclaim Wonderland for good. To be the ruler he had been born to be.

But then his gaze shifted to Ellie, whose skin became paler by the second. With her eyes closed, her long eyelashes cast shadows across her delicate cheekbones and dusting of freckles across her skin. He recalled what she'd said a short time ago. Magic-wielders could live for a short time without their heart, but should it be destroyed, even they could not survive such a fate.

Something plopped onto her cheek, and he wiped it away with a careful hand, only for a second to take its place.

However, when a third appeared, shock engulfed him when he lifted his fingers to his face to find wet tears trailing from the corners of his eyes. They refused to stop, so he ceased swiping them away and gazed down through blurred vision at the dying woman he held tenderly in his arms.

The heat rapidly dissipated from her limp body. The once rosy hue of her cheeks gradually faded.

As if he could still find that warmth, he dared to lift a hand to her face, caressing the cold, soft skin with the back of his finger. It was as if at any moment, she might open those dark brown eyes of hers and scowl at him before giving him a snarky tongue thrashing.

But her eyes remained closed. There was no such scowl.

Yes, she may have been immortal, but her heart had been shattered to shards of dust that no amount of magic could revive.

"Ellie," he whispered her name, hoping against hope for her to open her eyes.

She didn't.

Several more tears blurred her image before he pulled her closer to rest his forehead against hers. This was his fated person. He'd wildly denied it again and again, but now that no more time remained...

He realized he'd lost her. Fate had a cruel way of playing the most malicious jokes.

"Ellie," he murmured again, lightly brushing his fingers against her hair. "Telly, jelly, felly, smelly. Scratch that last one. You actually smell quite nice." He laughed miserably and squeezed his eyes shut. Two rivers of emotion skippered down his face.

He hated this feeling. Of losing control. Not of his magic, but of his heart. A sorceress. Someone who had cursed princesses to dance all night but who had always longed to dance herself. Someone who had desired to be loved that she'd fought for so long against the impossible. A gardener who had snarked her way into his life, though she was terrible at taking care of his roses after all. Caught lying on her resume.

Another miserable laugh escaped him. What he wouldn't do for her to destroy his entire garden with her black thumb, if only to trade it for the smirk on her lips and the shock in her eyes every time he said something dumb.

But he'd realized too late. The spade on his wrist... The heart on hers...

It didn't matter anymore.

"I'm sorry," he whispered before placing a long, lingering kiss on her forehead and then blinked back a couple more tears until his vision cleared enough to spot the light freckles on her face. "I hope you at least find solace knowing that someone loved you."

After slipping Alice's metallic glove over his fingers, he held Ellie gently in one arm while lifting the Heart of Wonderland in his other hand. The crystal pulsed with a steady light. "Take care of Wonderland for me."

And then he shoved his own heart into her chest, and the earth quaked mightily in recognition of its new queen.

A Mad Leap of Faith

The entire world shook. The walls trembled. The floor quaked. Warmth burned hot inside Ellie's chest, incredibly uncomfortable at first until the heat trickled down to a small flame. The pain in her abdomen and foot subsided as the warmth healed her body. Strength flooded through her.

Along with panic.

Because although she was no longer unconscious and dying because of the destruction of her heart, Rylan was still missing his, the very heart that beat inside her own chest.

"Rylan Rhapsody!" Alice screeched from where she lay on the ground clutching her shoulder. "You deserve death for everything you've done. You're a tyrant! Tyrants need to be cleansed from the earth."

Deathly pale and on the verge of collapse, Rylan stumbled to his feet and braced himself against the wall. "Everything I've done is for the good of the kingdom. And perhaps the more questionable things… I'll never get the chance to right my wrongs and do better. But also…maybe you won't either."

Rylan's knees collapsed at that moment, and Ellie rushed forward to catch him, leaning him heavily against her shoulder.

Alice screeched again, but the scream was cut off as she shrank down into a small black rabbit, sniffing as she hopped around idly as if she'd lost her mind the moment of the transformation. But Ellie couldn't be bothered when Rylan was still dying beside her, at a more rapid rate than before.

She had his heart. And she couldn't give it back. Although it was powerful, beating with such resonating magic within her chest, it wasn't magic she could access. Not without the sigil blockage flowing through her blood.

"Hold on, Rylan," she murmured, trying to catch her bearings and pushing away the growing panic within her. "I can save you. I know how to save you. But we have to get to the upper world. Hold on until then. Promise me."

Rylan only grunted, more of his weight pressed against her as if he struggled for consciousness.

Unlike the last trap she'd missed, which had resulted in their unfortunate fall, she recognized the lever behind the stone altar as a mechanism to open a doorway. Instead of the floor swallowing them whole, when she pulled the lever, a stone door rumbled open on the opposite end of the room.

Quickly, she rushed through the doorway as fast as Rylan's stumbling feet could keep up with her. They traveled down several stone corridors, and when the path forked both left and right, she chose the right when the faintest whistle of wind beckoned her forward.

Nothing else mattered right now other than getting Rylan to safety. Although Alice was now a harmless rabbit, Ellie now needed to worry about her soldiers.

At the end of the tunnel lay a metal gate, a gap just large enough to fit a person through the bars. She slid through first and maneuvered Rylan through second. He barely managed to stumble after her, his eyes hooded as if he might collapse at any moment.

"Just a little farther," she encouraged with a squeeze to his arm now looped around her neck. "Don't collapse on me yet. Just hold on."

"Leave me," Rylan grunted as they stumbled outside in the fresh air outside the fortress with the sunset glistening through the trees. "I'm not long for this world, anyway."

"Ridiculous!" she hissed, tightening her grip around his waist when her fingers kept slipping. "I'm a nobody sorceress. You're the King of Hearts. Why would you do something like this?"

He chuckled but then grimaced as if the action pained him. "Why, indeed?"

His body became even more limp against her. Panic spurred her faster, but his stumbling prevented her from walking as quickly as she wanted.

Shouts of soldiers echoed behind her while the snort of horses sounded in front of her. They were almost there. So close now.

Their horses came into view, one flicking its tail nervously and slightly rearing back on its hind legs as if it sensed danger. She untied the horse from a branch and smacked its rear. It needed no encouragement to gallop away from them and disappear down the path in a plume of dirt kicking up in its wake.

"You have to help me," Ellie grunted as she attempted to help Rylan into the saddle of the remaining horse. "I can't lift you."

Somehow, between the two of them, they managed to get Rylan in the saddle while she clambered up behind him and held on tight. More shouts echoed at the fortress. She wasted no more time as she kicked the horse's flanks, and the creature thundered forward on racing hooves.

Wind whipped through Ellie's hair. Trees snagged at her clothes. A protruding branch scratched her temple as they galloped, but she never lost focus on the road ahead.

Although she couldn't see it as easily beneath the sunset light, she located the faint shimmer of the Staircase to Nowhere in the distance. If she were to heal him, she needed her magic back. And the only way to make sure he didn't keel over before she managed the feat was to bring him with her.

Rylan soon became limp in her arms. Without a heart beating in his chest, she couldn't feel for a pulse. But when she heard a raspy breath escape his mouth, she knew he was still alive.

Hold on, she silently begged. *Just hold on a little longer.*

It seemed to take forever and a half to reach the staircase located in the middle of a forest clearing surrounded by bright, leafy trees a variety of colors in the rainbow. Red leaves, blue leaves, green, purple, orange, yellow, and even pink.

The horse slowed to a trot, and before the creature managed a full stop, Ellie hopped down and pulled Rylan after her. It took all her effort to keep him from flopping onto the ground in his unconscious state. The disguise had worn off, and his normal black curls and tan skin had returned.

Gritting her teeth, she glanced toward the winding staircase that traveled up, up, up and disappeared into the clouds above. There was no railing. Nothing to catch her should she fall. If she misstepped, they would both plummet to the earth and lose their lives.

The staircase wasn't wide enough to fit a horse. She would have to do this on her own.

Internally counting down from three, she twisted her body and hefted Rylan up on her shoulders. A grunt of exertion escaped her, and it felt as if the weight of him was crushing her lungs.

She couldn't do this. He was too heavy.

But she had to. No other choice remained.

That first step on the staircase threatened to collapse her. She took a deep, struggling breath and tightened her grip on Rylan. Just a thousand more steps to go. No big deal.

She took another step, followed by another, taking one step at a time. Little by little. It was possible. She could do this.

Each breath became uncomfortably labored the moment she crested the top of the tree line. However, the staircase still stretched upward and upward some more. Where was that giant when she needed it? Perhaps it could have given her a lift out of Wonderland with a stretch of its hand.

Sunset colors splashed against the shimmering, near-translucent stairs beneath her feet. She forced herself to keep her gaze on the stairs in front of her rather than the earth growing smaller beneath her.

Her legs wobbled. Each breath escaped as a gasp. With each passing moment, her strength waned.

Then she made the mistake of glancing up.

The stairs stretched endlessly above her with no end in sight. They kept going and going until what appeared to be the end disappeared into a flickering star. The ground lay far below her, the forest sprawled across one end of the horizon to the other. She wasn't sure how, but she'd already climbed so high. How much farther was her destination?

Rylan's words came to mind. *Just when you think there's no end in sight, you're a quarter of the way there!*

"Idiot king!" she gasped, stumbling on her own feet and teetering far too close to the edge. "You should have been more specific!"

Immediately, she regretted wasting what precious breath remained in her lungs. She took another step, but her leg collapsed beneath her. She barely managed to catch herself on the next stair, but hers and Rylan's legs draped precariously over the edge. Even one wrong breath might topple them over the side.

She clawed her way back to her feet and repositioned Rylan over her shoulders. Little strength remained in her body. She couldn't do it. She couldn't do it!

Yet, she took another step. Her other leg threatened to give out, shaking with the effort to keep herself from falling again.

She only made it three more stairs before her lungs could no longer find enough capacity to draw any more air. A sob of desperation escaped her mouth, the pitiful sound of someone who knew they had lost. Rylan had sacrificed his own heart to save her. And she couldn't even return the favor.

She didn't want his sacrifice to end like this. She didn't want to lose him!

Gripping Rylan's limp hand in her own, she attempted to keep going, to move forward. But she couldn't even lift her leg. Her body refused to cooperate.

There has to be something! she cried in her mind. She tried to reach for the magic of the Heart of Wonderland. Rylan had taken off its seal, but she couldn't access it. It seemed only someone currently capable of magic could use it. No matter how hard she tried, it refused to obey her.

When her attempts failed, she tried to reach for Rylan's magic instead despite her knowing magic didn't transfer like that. It, too, refused to obey her.

She was destitute. Alone. Powerless.

And now? Only one choice remained—to climb back down. Because the only other option was to leave him, and she couldn't do such a thing, not even for her own selfish gains.

But as she glanced down the staircase, she realized how high she'd climbed. Either she needed to carry him or drag him down step by step, risking injuring him or worse.

"I'm so sorry, Rylan," she whispered, tears trailing from her eyes and down her cheeks. Her vision blurred. Her breath staggered. Never had she thought she'd discover what it truly meant to love someone. For someone to care for her enough to sacrifice his very heart and life for her. And now? She'd lost it all.

She tipped her head upward, tears falling off her chin while the shimmering staircase blurred into small streams of colorful light. Hopelessness weighed on her soul. If she couldn't save the man she loved, then what else mattered?

Suddenly, her eyes flew open as she gasped. This was the Stairway to Nowhere. A destination didn't exist on the other side of the staircase. Rather, the destination was wherever you were going. That's what Rylan had said.

This was *Wonderland*. Not the world she was from. She had to trust in the strange and abnormal, pushing away everything that made sense to her and rejecting the sane.

She recalled Rylan's words. *"To find your way, sometimes you must lose yourself."* Therefore, she gave up trying to follow the rules of her own land and let everything she had ever known wash away. If going upward was nowhere, then going nowhere was somewhere. She must try something else.

So, taking a mad leap of faith, she closed her eyes and leaned backward, trusting in the abnormal, in the insane. Her entire body and Rylan's pivoted over the edge of the staircase. And they fell downward through the Wonderland abyss.

A Snow so White

Wind whipped through Ellie's hair. Her stomach dropped. Her heart leaped to her throat. She held on tightly to Rylan, not daring to let go for a single moment.

And then her body flipped upside down. Light became dark. Dry became wet. Warm became chilly. The scent of humidity filled the air.

The earth turned violently, and they slammed upside down, hitting the soft but cold earth with a thud, Rylan landing on top of her.

Ellie groaned from the impact and struggled to push him off her. "I suppose I deserved that," she said with a cough, rubbing her aching ribs. That's when she finally noticed her surroundings.

She lay in the darkness of night, staring up at a sky filled with dark gray clouds tinged with a deep orange, signaling an approaching snowfall. The dark silhouette of pine trees surrounded her. A still silence filled the air.

Pushing herself up on her elbows, her heart thudded hard in her chest when she recognized the area around her. A meadow void of wildflowers in the late fall. Tall pine trees. The scent of wet bark in the air.

This was the upper world.

Not just that, but this was home.

Ellie scrambled to her feet, hope taking flight in her chest. Amidst the pine trees and dark clouds was the silhouette of a lone cottage in the woods. Home. She was home.

She stooped next to Rylan and placed a hand on his chest. Although no heartbeat echoed back against her fingers, his chest rose and fell with each breath. He was still alive. But only barely. The castle was too far away to reach from here without the help of proper transportation. She wouldn't get her magic back today, but she could still prolong Rylan's life for just a little while longer.

Fueled with renewed hope, she lay down in the crook of Rylan's arm and draped his other arm across her. Using all the strength remaining in her body, she rolled onto her feet, using the momentum to pick Rylan up and drape him across her shoulders one more time.

Step by step, she carted him across frozen earth and toward the rectangular silhouette growing larger by the second. Finally, she reached her cottage and pushed open the door. It creaked from the lack of usage for many weeks, leading into the humble abode within. The cottage was only one semi-spacious room with a cot tucked against the wall, an empty fireplace on the adjacent wall, a small dining table in the middle covered in dried herbs and dying plants, and a small clothesline draped in the corner with the few dresses she owned hanging from it.

"Over two hundred years old and this is all I can manage?" she murmured to herself, embarrassed.

She carefully placed Rylan on the cot, lit a fire in the hearth to illuminate and warm up the room, and immediately got to work with her herbs and other magical items she'd collected over the years.

Every now and again, she'd glance up to make sure Rylan still breathed as she worked. Every passing minute created more of a labored rasp with each of his breaths. He was dying. But she hadn't made it this far just to lose him now.

She quickened her pace until she created a magical remedy with ingredients for dark magic. Without her own magic working as it should, she was limited in what she could do. But with a few sprinkles of herbs and other ingredients collected from the Dark Wood, she could still prolong his life.

By giving up some of her own.

It was only two days off her total immortal lifespan, but it was enough to get Rylan the help he needed. It *had* to be enough. And if it wasn't, she'd shave off a few more days. Months or years if necessary. He meant a lot to her. She refused to play the stingy sorceress now.

Approaching the cot, she placed her hand behind Rylan's neck and lifted his head to help him drink. Some of the elixir dribbled out of the corner of his mouth, but most of it remained inside. Even in his unconscious state, it was almost as if his body recognized her attempts to help. He swallowed little by little until the bowl lay empty.

Then after she set his head back down, she waited.

It only took a minute before he gasped in a sharp breath, coughed, and blinked his eyes open.

Ellie's heart shuddered with relief. Emotion burned behind her eyes. He was alive. If he could hold on only a couple more days, she was sure she could regain her magic and save him entirely.

"Am I dead?" he asked, his voice coming out as little more than a rasp as he glanced around the room with a disoriented expression. "It tastes like death here."

She rolled her eyes but couldn't stop a relieved chuckle from escaping her mouth. "This is the upper realm."

"Bleh. No wonder."

Rather than the retort that might have escaped on another day, she laughed, the sound wet from her pesky emotions. For a moment, she'd thought she was going to lose him. Of course, she still could. But she'd bought him just a little bit more time.

She reached out to him and placed a hand against his cheek, drawing his attention back to her. His eyes appeared tired but lucid. The color, although still pale, had mostly returned to his face.

"How..." He took a deep breath and let it out slowly, wincing as if the action pained him. "How did I get here? Where...where are we?"

When she recounted their arduous escape on horseback and then their adventure up the Stairway to Nowhere, he stared back at her in disbelief. And when she finally ended the tale of reaching her cottage home, he looked at her with a foreign emotion she'd never seen directed at her before. It was soft. Gentle. Warm.

"A lone cottage in the woods?" he replied at last. "You're really living up to your sorceress stereotype."

"I thought you might appreciate that," she jested back.

"Immensely. Now you must show me your cauldron and the cages where you keep trapped children."

She rolled her eyes and pinched his side, no longer wary of touching him. Surprise filled his handsome features at first, but then a slow smile crept across his lips.

"You carried me all the way here," he seemed to realize. "And you're still alive."

"Mmhmm. You're not as dangerous as you seem to think you are."

"But I..." He trailed off, his eyes filled to the brim with confusion. "I've hurt others in the past."

Trying to show she wasn't afraid of him, she pulled off his gloves and gripped his hands tightly. "You have exercised practice and careful control through your roses. You are more in control of your magic than you think. You can't hurt me." Her mouth quirked to the side. "Unless you purposefully try, of course."

"I would never."

She closed her eyes and breathed out a contented sigh. "I know."

After a few moments, his teasing and levity returned at full force. "You're still holding my hands." She tried to pull away, but his grip on her tightened. "No. I like it. A lot. Don't let me go."

"Then I won't."

What a strange turn of events, she thought to herself as the crackles and pops of the hearth filled the cottage with a cozy, happy atmosphere. At the time, she'd thought exile to the Mad Lands was the absolute worst punishment she could receive. In hindsight, it had been one of the best things to have happened to her. She'd made friends. She'd found purpose in her life. And she'd met Rylan.

Perhaps going mad wasn't as terrible as everyone else made it out to be.

"You're not what I expected," Rylan said finally, breaking the warm, comfortable silence between them. He played with her fingers, fascination in his expression as if he'd never seen or touched another pair of hands before. His thumb brushed against the sigil on one wrist with black spikes striking through a circle. He only stared at the other mark on her opposite wrist, the shape of a red heart.

"What do you mean?"

He stared down at her hands for a long moment before lifting his gaze. His expression seemed almost shy, completely taking her back. Rylan was usually anything but shy.

"The mark on your wrist," he murmured, only now brushing his thumb against the red heart. "It matches mine." He flipped his hand to show her a black spade on his wrist, the same size and placement as her own. And then he took a deep breath. "You're my fated person. I'm glad it was you."

She blinked slowly, trying to figure out what he meant by his words. Fated person? Like…like…a soulmate?

A sudden blush stole across her cheeks, warming her against the chilly weather barking at her door. Ever since she'd discovered the heart symbol, she'd assumed it was a curse mark just like the other. But… A mark of fate? She'd only ever heard stories of such marks.

"It's not a curse mark?"

He chuckled but then coughed. She rushed across the room to ladle cold stream water into a cup and returned to his side to help him drink. After a few sips, he answered.

"Depends on how you look at it. Is being fatefully shackled to me a curse or something else entirely?" Although his words sounded nonchalant, he glanced at her from the corner of his eye and waited anxiously for her answer.

She smiled into her lap, the warmth in her face still searing her cheeks. "It only costs me a few headaches. But…such a fate doesn't sound so terrible."

Lifting her gaze, she found Rylan's eyes flashing mischievously. "Then you must kiss me to seal our fate."

Her heart leaped to her throat, her gaze flickering to his lips. But she thought she recognized the nearly imperceptible teasing smirk at the corner of his mouth. She lightly smacked his shoulder.

"Make it through the night first, and then I can see what I can do."

He let out a long, pitiful sigh and gave her a pout. "You already have my heart. What more do you want?"

The double meaning came across loud and clear. Yes, his heart beat inside her chest. But did he also mean…

Did he return her feelings?

Before she managed to ponder on it further, he grimaced and lifted a hand to his temple. She pressed her hand to his forehead, inhaling sharply at the heat of a fever warming her fingers. This wasn't good. Her magical concoction may have extended his life, but it wouldn't necessarily ease his suffering.

His eyes glazed over. Hot breaths escaped his mouth. His eyebrows pinched together as if pained.

Over the next several hours, Rylan flitted in and out of consciousness as his fever waxed and waned. One moment, he would open lucid eyes, but then the next, his gaze would appear far away.

She cooled his fever with wet cloths and forced him to drink water, even when he fought against her efforts. If he could make it through the night, she was sure she could find a way to get him to the castle where she'd been cursed. As a last resort, she could go herself. But despite her sacrifice of two days from her own immortal lifespan, she couldn't guarantee that whatever sickness plagued him wouldn't take him sooner while she was gone.

After hours of effort, she blinked her eyes open following a short nap to find Rylan squinting at the wall, seemingly half-conscious. Behind him, the darkness of midnight revealed itself from the window, as well as the one thing she knew Rylan had never seen.

"Look, Rylan," she whispered, gently turning his head toward the window and the flurry of powder brushing against the glass. "Snow."

"Snow?" he croaked, his half-lidded eyes blinking rapidly as if he struggled to focus on the windowpanes. But then a smile slowly lifted on his lips. "I have never…seen snow…before."

"Just you wait." She brushed his temple with a cool cloth. "Once you feel better, stand outside and gaze up at the sky. You'll feel as if you're in a snow globe." Her thumb caressed the black curls clinging to the side of his head. "Now rest."

But before he managed a reply, wood splintered as someone kicked open the front door with no warning. Moments later, guards dressed in black armor marched inside.

King Melgren's guards.

Ellie shot to her feet and spread her arms out on either side of her, a weak attempt to protect Rylan from the men who likely wanted her dead.

"By order of King Melgren the fourth," one of the guards said, his hand resting on his hilt, "you, Sorceress Ellie Strife, are hereby arrested for resisting your sentence and will be placed on trial on the morrow." He cleared his throat and glanced over Ellie's shoulder. "You and your accomplice," he amended.

"He's innocent!" she shouted. "Just take me! I'm the one you want." She rushed to stand in front of Rylan, but the guards grabbed either of her arms and restrained her.

The men took one look at Rylan and nodded to each other. "He's decrepit. Leave him for now."

The room quieted suddenly, and everyone stared at the Mad King as he shakily climbed to his feet and faced all of them, even with a worn expression and exhaustion in the hunch of his shoulders.

Rylan pointed at one of the guards, a mischievous lift on the corner of his mouth. "You are ugly. And your breath smells. I'll spit on your king." He paused before adding. "Curse this kingdom."

When one of the guards' hands grew slack around her arm in their shock, Ellie smacked herself in the forehead moments before the guards arrested Rylan in earnest, binding him with a rope behind his back. Couldn't he just let her get detained on her own without having to involve himself? Always wanting to be the center of attention. Ridiculous king.

Together, they were dragged outside, shoved into the back of a wagon pulled by two horses, and surrounded by six guards on horseback. The driver whipped the horses into movement. The wagon lurched forward on squeaky wheels with very little light to guide them except for the drifts of white snow fluttering down from the skies in the dim light of early morning.

"You're right!" Rylan gasped across from her. "It does look like a snow globe."

"No talking," one of the guards warned.

Rylan grinned. "What a difficult concept to comprehend. I'm not sure I can manage the feat. You may have to gag me first."

"That can be arranged."

"Rylan!" Ellie warned. She'd prefer him ungagged in case something went very wrong. Melgren was likely to sentence her to something even worse than mere exile. By association with her, Rylan might not fare any better.

Across the wagon, Rylan met her eye with a playful glint in his expression that seemed to say, *Isn't this fun? I'm having fun.*

She released a breathy chuckle and rolled her eyes at him. There was no such thing as a cloudy day for this man. He was someone who managed to take all the bumps in the road with an optimistic attitude.

She loved that about him.

Her attention turned upward to the snow drifting down from the skies, each flake dancing and twirling and spinning. Just like a snow globe. The flakes were large and gentle. The night was quiet and lovely despite the current situation.

Ellie lowered her gaze from the skies to find snowflakes in Rylan's hair and on the tips of his eyelashes. Absolute wonder lived in his expression, the softness in his eyes making him look even more beautiful beneath the waning darkness.

With a gentle blink, his gaze met hers across the wagon. Flutters filled her stomach in the most pleasant way. The quiet affection in his eyes. The faintest smile at the corner of his lips. They'd been through so much together already. And for their fun and terrifying adventures to lead them here to this moment?

It truly was fate.

With her hands tied awkwardly behind her, her thumb brushed against the red heart on her wrist while she never broke eye contact with him. After two hundred and fifty years, fate had brought her here. To him. And she never wanted to leave.

Rylan cleared his throat and held himself straighter. "I'd like to make an official decree!" he called out, his voice loud in the darkness.

"Shut it, prisoner!" A guard kicked the wagon in response to the outburst, but Rylan seemed undeterred.

"From this day onward," he called out, still in a loud, kingly voice, "let it be known that King Rylan Rhapsody of Wonderland has fallen mad in love with the Sorceress Ellie, Queen of Spades and most wonderful woman to exist in the entire—"

"That's it! You're getting a gag." A guard quickly produced a strip of cloth and bound Rylan's mouth with it, but not before the Mad King managed a flirtatious grin in her direction.

Ellie's heart thumped hard in her chest, unbearable heat filling her entire body and chasing away the cold nip in the air. She stared back at Rylan with wide, disbelieving eyes, momentarily at a loss for words—and thoughts for that matter. There was no trace of a jest in his eyes. Only warmth and mirth and…and…

Love.

Her heart flipped and flopped and fluttered. But then she realized it wasn't truly her heart, was it? It was Rylan's. To have given her such a precious gift at the expense of himself…

"I-I-I'm a lot older than you," she protested in her fluster.

Rylan simply gave her an unapologetic shrug when he couldn't speak with a gagged mouth.

"I-I-I'm a sorceress."

He struggled against his bindings for a moment before giving up and shrugging again. He clearly wanted to say something, but she tried to read his expressions instead.

It doesn't matter, he seemed to say, followed by another soft look in those gold eyes of his.

Ellie wanted to sob in relief, in happiness, and she barely managed to hold back her emotions. To have someone she loved return her feelings? She'd never thought it was possible. Then again, he didn't have to say the words for her to know the truth. He'd danced with her beneath moon-lit windows. He'd carried her when she was too injured to stand. He'd sacrificed his own heart to keep her alive.

He loved her.

And she needed him to know the workings of her own heart as well.

"I'd like to make a decree!" Ellie shouted. All the guards groaned while one of them also produced a gag. The man steered his horse around the cart and reached for her. She tried to get the words out quickly. "From this day onward, let it be known that Sorceress Ellie Strife of the upper world has fallen mad in love with King Rylan Rhapsody, King of Hearts—"

The guard gagged her as well, muffling her last words before she managed to utter the rest. However, across from her, Rylan's entire face lit up with unbridled joy. He reached forward with his foot and rested the tip of his shoe against her own. It was all they could do. No other words needed to be spoken. This was enough.

Rylan waggled his eyebrows at her and nodded his head toward one of the guards. Despite the silence forced between them, she could almost hear him say, *I could take this man out. How good are you at riding a horse without any hands?*

Imperceptibly, she shook her head. They were on their way to exactly where they wanted to go. It was best if they waited out this situation.

And then a pit of dooming despair filled her soul when she spotted the silhouette of the Elyrian castle in the distance, bringing with it a sense of mixed emotions. Every time she'd seen it in the past, it used to inspire hatred and longing and injustice. But now?

Now she wanted to flee from it. To put it behind her. To escape its looming shadow. What if she could never escape? What if the shadow followed her for the rest of her life?

Rylan's shoe knocked against hers, and she glanced toward him to find reassurance and comfort in his gaze. *You're not alone*, he seemed to say. *I'll be with you every step of the way.*

She took a deep breath and let it out slowly. It was time to confront her past. It seemed like a lifetime ago. And perhaps it was. But now she must face the consequences of her actions.

Where was a comforting rackleberry tart when she needed one?

We're All a Bit Mad Here

Rylan felt as if he were standing at the edge of the sky, euphoria raining down on him like warm rays of sunshine.

Ellie loved him. She'd proclaimed it to the world. And now? Everything else was trivial in comparison. This gag, this wagon, these soldiers. Nothing else mattered except the woman sitting across from him.

Even as the wagon passed beneath a black steel gate, not a single worry crossed his mind. If anything, this was just another interesting adventure they would one day tell their children about.

He smiled at the thought. He'd never imagined a future with a wife and children. But now? He had every reason to daydream about the possibility.

The wagon groaned to a jolting halt just as the morning daylight crept into the sky, much to his fascination. The sun rose on its own without a giant batting it around in the sky. The concept was so strange and foreign to him. He found it unnerving and difficult to wrap his mind around.

One after the other, the guards hauled them off the wagon and into an outdoor courtyard riddled with guards watching Ellie with wary eyes. They seemed to know her and understand what she was capable of. Just what kind of mischief had his darling sorceress been up to before they'd met?

Several guards restrained Ellie by the arms, and just the sight of them touching her boiled his blood into a heated frenzy. How dare they lay a hand on her!

"I would release her if I were you!" Rylan shouted, his voice muffled by the gag tied around his mouth.

One of the guards decorated with a variety of metal pins on his uniform laughed and shook his head. "Lock him up in the dungeon. We'll deal with him later."

At the man's command, several men approached with weapons drawn.

With a twist of his head, the gag fell from Rylan's mouth to reveal his accompanying grin. "I have one thing I want to say first..." The guards glanced toward him, at least twelve surrounding them now. "Have you ever met a kneazle?"

Peachy Puff leaped out from the confines of Rylan's shirt and hopped onto the ground near his feet. The guards blinked confusedly at the small creature, all while Ellie smiled widely around the gag holding her mouth captive. For someone who had feared kneazles only weeks ago, she sure was excited to see one now.

"Ignore him," the main guard said. "Take him to the dungeon. And get rid of that...creature."

Just as the guards stepped toward Rylan, Peachy Puff transformed from his sweet, innocent form into one more beastly and terrifying. The little thing grew larger in size, sharp teeth shooting out of its mouth while a ravenous hunger flashed across its eyes.

One of the guards let out a high-pitched scream, followed by the clattering of metal as he fainted to the ground. And then chaos erupted as Peachy Puff attacked.

Guards shouted and wildly swung their weapons, but the kneazle moved too quickly and easily dodged each attack. The creature jumped forward and latched its sharp teeth around one of the men's legs.

More chaos and screaming.

Ellie, now free of her captors' grip, chose that moment to dart forward and bump her shoulder into Rylan's. Together, they sprinted in the opposite direction and slipped into the castle through an unguarded door. They stopped only for a moment for her to catch her gag on the handle of a door and pull it off her face.

"I had no idea you still carried Peachy Puff around!" she gasped before they turned their backs to one another. With awkwardly restrained fingers, he untied the rope from her hands. Once the rope came loose, she more easily unbound him before they continued running forward.

"How could I not smuggle my little pet around? He's too adorable!"

They linked their fingers together. "Let's go! The ballroom should be around the corner."

When the chaos of the courtyard resounded behind them, the hallways lay mostly empty aside from the early morning servants scurrying to find out what the fuss was about. She led Rylan by the hand down several corridors before they pushed open the heavy double doors leading into the ballroom where she'd been cursed that fateful night.

Where she'd tried to curse Melgren and his family.

Looking back now, she realized how ridiculous her obsession had been. How blind and small-minded. But now? All she wanted was to retrieve her magic and leave with Rylan. Without having to kill the curse's caster.

"This was the place," she murmured, glancing around the spacious room with the enormous chandelier now hidden in the shadows of the ceiling. It had felt like such a long time ago since she'd been here. To think she'd changed so much since her last visit.

"Wait a minute!" Rylan cried while holding up a single finger. "I must change my outfit for this momentous occasion." He ducked behind a long blue curtain hanging from the ceiling to apparently change out of his borrowed clothing from earlier.

"You brought your clothes with you?" she asked in disbelief.

"Of course, I did!" He peeked only his head out and gave her an adorable, innocent expression. "I stashed them in my portable greenhouse. Do you think I planned to wear these dreadful Tweedle Dee threads for any longer than necessary?"

"Hurry then. The guards will catch up any minute." She glanced toward the door. No one chased after them yet. She only hoped Peachy Puff wouldn't get hurt from all the commotion.

"Done!" Rylan said, sweeping the curtain aside and striding forward in a kingly ensemble. A black vest over a white shirt beneath. A black cape over his right shoulder. A crown inlaid with red heart rubies. And…no gloves.

Her heart unexpectedly warmed at the sight.

He followed her to the middle of the room where she remembered failing to cast a curse on King Melgren. It was as if an invisible thread pulled her in, directing her on where to go. The curse mark on her wrist pulsed with every step as if sensing the cage was nearly unlocked. If Rylan was correct about how apparently simple it was to expel a curse, then the end was finally near.

She stepped onto the exact tile on the floor where she'd fallen prey to the curse. Her wrist pulsed harder like a heartbeat within her veins.

Slowly, the curse mark on her wrist disappeared, fading little by little until not a single trace of it remained. It was as if a cage unlatched within her soul, and her magic flooded out, filling every available crevice within her in eager anticipation. A large missing piece of her returned. Finally, she felt whole. Complete.

She lifted her hand, silvery magic threading through her fingers. It snaked around her hand and her wrist. Waiting for her to call upon it. Now that her magic had returned…

"Touch my hand," she instructed Rylan.

However, he only leaned closer and suspiciously eyed the silver magic clinging to her fingers. "What does it do?"

"What I will it to, energy and magic supply willing." Again, she gestured with her fingers for him to comply. "Hearts are meant to be shared."

His eyes widened when he seemed to catch her meaning. But instead of stepping forward, he took a giant step backward. "I cannot risk you getting hurt."

"And you think I want to watch you wither away?"

He shook his head. "You don't understand what you're asking. This is the Heart of Wonderland. It's never been shared before. Splitting it could be disastrous. It could kill you and me and destroy this entire kingdom. And then Wonderland would fall soon after. I'm not sure I want to take such a risk."

"Well, I, for one, do. I'll take any risk." She looked him in the eye, her gaze gentle and reassuring.

"You have less on the line."

"I disagree. You are worth more than any kingdom." Her cheeks heated at such a confession, the burn only worsening at the dumbstruck look in Rylan's eyes. To say she'd sacrifice two entire kingdoms in exchange for his life… Well, that was no small thing.

Finally, he approached with a nonchalant swagger to his step. "You better know what you're doing."

"Ha... Of course I do..."

The nervous twitch of his mouth told her he'd detected her hesitation. But he lifted his hand to hers, finger to finger, palm to palm, and chose to trust her anyway. She was going to save his life. By sharing what life he had already given to her.

Taking a deep breath, she closed her eyes and allowed her magic to flow into the Heart of Wonderland in her chest, up her arm, through where their fingers touched, and into Rylan's body. Rather than splitting directly down the middle, the heart fused their souls together. The heart beat strongly for both of them. As one. Shared between them. An echo of love, trust, and responsibility.

Rylan's face once more found its color. The strength returned to the set of his shoulders. Energy and radiance burst to life within his eyes, *their* heart beating strongly between them.

All too suddenly, Rylan dropped his hand and placed his fists on his hips, looking at the ceiling, at the floor, before finally settling on his sleeves.

"Well!" he coughed, brushing down his clothing and looking anywhere but at her. "No wonder we received fated marks. We're good and stuck together now. What a shame. What a shame." He glanced at her out of the corner of his eye, a teasing mirth shining in his expression.

She sighed, playing along. "Whatever will I do now? I don't believe this heart will allow me to remain in a different realm while its other half tarries in another."

He lifted his hand to inspect his nails. "It seems there is no other choice. You must return to Wonderland with me."

A sly grin pulled on her lips. "What a shame, indeed."

"But there can't be two unrelated monarchs on the throne," he added, now inspecting his other set of nails. "We must do something about that."

"Naturally."

"A large, momentous occasion, of course."

"With plenty of roses."

"And tea! Don't forget the tea."

They'd both clasped each other's hands, fingers woven together. Ellie gazed back at the mischief permanently etched into the gold of his eyes and couldn't help but smile. The last thing she had expected when getting banished to Wonderland was him. Little had she known... He was the very thing she'd needed the most.

"If we dally any longer," Rylan murmured, "someone's bound to catch us making eyes at each other. Now, how am I supposed to explain that?"

She laughed and pulled him by the hand in the opposite direction. "Let's leave. Quickly."

But before they managed another step, a man in his sixties wearing a crown and kingly robes strode into the room with a furious expression between knitted brows. He lifted a finger and pointed toward them.

"Guards!" King Melgren shouted. "Surround them!"

Men wearing armor filed into the room with swords drawn, a few appearing wary after what had happened with Peachy Puff. The kneazle in question jumped between legs and armor in its cutsie form and leaped onto Rylan's shoulder. Although the men surrounded them, none dared to get too close with their guard animal silently baring its teeth.

"This is him?" Rylan whispered, leaning closer to her. "The man you obsessed decades over?"

She rolled her eyes, realizing how ridiculous the situation was after the fact. "Shut it."

"I'm far better looking than him."

She elbowed him in the ribs. "Save the teasing for later."

Melgren's stride slowed as he glanced between them, his gaze lingering longer on Rylan. The King of Hearts exuded the aura of a king, which was likely what made Melgren pause and approach warily.

Rylan lifted Ellie's hand and kissed her knuckles. "I'll handle this, love."

Ellie pinched the bridge of her nose, waiting for the coming headache to rush over her. Whatever came out of Rylan's mouth next was bound to leave a scorch mark across everyone's brain.

A large grin spread across Rylan's face as he whipped his cape to the side and offered a slight bow to the other king. "Rylan Rhapsody. King of Hearts. Sovereign of Wonderland." He straightened, his grin only growing larger at the shocked expression on King Melgren's face. He jerked his thumb over his shoulder toward Ellie. "You dumped a little something in my kingdom. Rude. Wonderland is not a dumping ground. You should have offered her as a gift instead. I would have gladly taken her off your hands."

Again, the King of Elyria glanced back and forth between them before dipping into a hasty bow as if finally recognizing Rylan's similar station. "I meant no offense. But what she's done—"

"I'm well aware of what she's done. And as you have rudely dumped her into my kingdom, you have given up all rights of her sentence to *me*. The fact that you have dragged her back here after giving up all jurisdiction to her is quite an insult to her, to me, and to the entirety of Wonderland."

"I..." King Melgren trailed off, complete bafflement in his old, weathered eyes. She wanted to laugh out loud, but she forced herself to hold it in. Who knew that Rylan was actually good at politics? She would never have guessed.

After he recovered from his confusion, King Melgren approached Ellie with a withered, pointed finger in her face. Rylan smacked it away, but it didn't deter the other king. "You are still my subject! You owe me penance for your actions in my kingdom. Exile to the Mad Lands clearly was not enough of a punishment. Fifty lashes! And imprison—"

"Actually, the restitution for jilting in Wonderland is one year of curse per child born." Rylan counted on his fingers. "It appears you have twelve daughters, no? My *Queen of Spades* is letting you off easy for the punishment you rightly deserve." He shrugged, holding up each pinky to finish off the number twelve on his fingers. "Or she could finish the curse. What, ten...eleven more years left?"

Melgren paled, once again glancing back and forth between them as if he realized he'd grossly misunderstood the situation he'd walked into. Ellie's heart warmed at Rylan's title for her, and she rubbed her thumb across the heart mark on her wrist to make sure it still lingered.

The Elyrian king quickly backtracked when he seemed to understand what she was to the King of Wonderland. "I think...I think Miss Strife has been more than generous."

"That's what I thought." The look of fear and a figurative tail between his legs was almost as satisfying as if he had smacked the old man about. Rylan stepped closer to her. "What do you propose, my dear? I leave the rest up to you."

Ellie tried not to wring her hands but ended up fidgeting with the hem of her sleeve instead. "I think it's best to stay out of each other's lives."

King Melgren released a long breath filled with obvious relief. "Yes, that would be best."

He clearly had no intention of apologizing to her. After fifty years and he'd still never expressed regret, he never would at this point. But that didn't mean she had to hold onto past resentfulness and injustice herself.

"I'm sorry for my part in your daughters' misfortunes." She dipped her head, face flaming with the shame of her past misdeeds. "It will never happen again."

He scowled at her. "It better not. And also—" But before he finished that last sentence, he glanced toward Rylan and fell strangely silent. She looked over her shoulder to find Rylan smiling innocently. *Too* innocently.

With one last dip of her head, she said, "I wish you well."

"And I wish you well."

Rylan clapped his hands together. "We'll be off then. After all, Wonderland waits for no one. Don't want to miss all the excitement."

With a lift of his hand, Melgren ordered the guards to step back and provide a path for them. No one attacked, no one stopped them, as they made their way out of the castle and continued farther down the path leading away from the heartache of her past. Peace settled in her soul. She finally felt like she could move forward with her life.

When the sun rose in the sky, and the palace became a speck in the distance, only then did Ellie confront the man beside her.

She placed a hand on her hip and turned to face him. "You made all that up. About the restitution for jilting."

"Never!" He placed a mockingly sincere hand against his chest. "I'm the King of Hearts. I can create laws as I wish. It was one hundred percent true."

She playfully bumped him with her hip and gave him a saucy look. "So, now what?"

"Now we go back to stealing hearts and locking away the key!"

Laughing, she rolled her eyes and looped her arm through his. "And the second option?"

His eyes softened, and he placed his hand on top of hers and turned to face her. The back of his fingers lightly skimmed against her cheek, his eyes burning with all the warmth and adoration of true love. "You stay in Wonderland with me."

"And risk turning batty like the rest of you?"

Deep laughter emanated from his mouth as he flipped her wrist over to reveal the red heart emblazoned on her skin. He lowered his head and kissed the very symbol to mark her as his. Their shared heart beat hard against her ribs, the workings of a blush rising in her cheeks.

"It's far too late for that, my dear." He lifted his shoulder cloak with one arm, shielding them from view of the rest of the world as he pulled her to him and kissed her, sealing their love and their future with the brush of his lips. "We're all a bit mad here." He whispered the words across her mouth between kisses.

A grin stretched across her face as she leaned back enough to look into his eyes, her hand resting on his chest. She felt their shared heart stutter when she traced his lips with the light touch of her finger. "Must be something in the air."

"Must be." And then he pulled her in for another kiss until the world faded away, and all that was left was the sweet fragrance of roses and the bright hope for a happy future.

Thirteen o'Clock

"Cheers to the bride and groom!" Gideon Glimmer shouted. Confetti cannons shot off plumes of colorful paper and finger-sized fairies that rained sparkles down on tables filled with cakes and tea and tarts to celebrate the new couple.

A group of five fairies circled Rylan and Ellie, bathing them in sparkling shimmers as they kissed for the twelfth time that wonderful day, officially branding them as husband and wife according to Wonderland traditions.

Ellie smiled into the kiss, a joy so great bursting to life inside her chest. When they broke apart, she gazed into the golden eyes of her Mad King, feeling so blessed to have been tossed down that rabbit hole that fateful day. Without it, she wouldn't have met Rylan. She wouldn't have met her Wonderland friends. Instead, she would have been stewing inside a cauldron of anger and resentment until her black heart ended up failing her one day.

This was a far better alternative.

As another Wonderland tradition, Gideon Glimmer placed a laurel wreath atop their heads. One by one, their friends approached and wove a flower into each of their crowns until their heads brimmed with sweet, floral aromas and a colorful display.

At a small table, Rylan poured them a helping of tea in a small teacup the size of half her palm. With faces bursting with smiles, they linked arms and drank the tea in a single gulp. She couldn't help but recall when Rylan had teased her about linking arms and drinking the wedding cups with him. To think it had actually come true in a way she had never expected.

Rylan lifted her hand to the sky and shouted toward the crowd witnessing the wedding traditions. "May I present my lovely bride. The Queen of Spades!"

Applause and whistles rippled around the courtyard decorated with roses seemingly stretching for miles. Ellie glanced over each face that she had come to love. Her friends. Her subjects.

Her husband…

After two hundred and fifty years, she finally felt like she had somewhere to belong. And as for her immortal life…

Her fate was up in the air now. With her own heart destroyed and now sharing the Heart of Wonderland with Rylan, she reckoned she'd lost her immortality and now faced a mortal future. But if there was any life she wanted to lose her immortality for…

It was this one. With Rylan. With whatever future fate decided to throw at them.

They celebrated well into the day and perhaps even into the night. She still couldn't tell what time it was when day had lasted for a week already.

As if attuned to her thoughts, Rylan placed a small box the size of her palm into her hand. "For you. It's time you have one of your own."

Excitement raced through her as she pulled on the red ribbon to free the box of its wrapping. She pulled the lid off. And her heart skipped inside her chest, warmth spreading through her body as she gazed down at a silver pocket watch connected to a sparkling chain seemingly made of crystal.

She carefully pulled out the pocket watch and dangled it by the chain, watching as the hands spun around and around until they landed on twelve past singing rhymes o'clock.

"Now you'll never get lost," Rylan murmured, dangling his own gold pocket watch next to hers. They beautifully complimented the other, a matching pair with the most exquisite design.

"They are pocket watches. Not compasses."

"Same thing."

Rolling her eyes, she playfully bumped him with her shoulder. But he took that moment to grab her hand and sneak her away from the party and into the castle's garden.

"Do you know what happens after the thirteenth kiss?" Rylan asked beneath an arch filled with blooming pink flowers, waggling his eyebrows suggestively.

"Knowing you, I cannot even begin to guess."

He wrapped an arm around her waist and pulled her close to whisper in her ear. "It binds us together until the clock strikes thirteen."

"But there is no thirteen on the clock."

His eyes sparkled with mischief. "Exactly. You are mine. Forever."

She gasped as he pulled her close beneath the arch. Before she could utter a teasing protest, he silenced her with a kiss. And then another. Until her legs became weak and the world turned upside down in the most pleasant way.

She snaked her arms up his chest, over his shoulders, and wrapped them around his neck, pulling him down. Closer. Until no space remained between them.

Their shared heart beat in sync, a happy, joyful rhythm full of sweet, tender longing. A loving bond so strong that it would take more than just death to sever it.

When they broke apart, her stomach fluttered pleasantly at the loving fondness in his eyes as he stroked her cheek with his thumb.

Wordlessly, he took both her hands and walked backward while leading her deeper into the garden. Although she didn't know where, exactly, he was going, she knew that after all their adventures together, she would follow him anywhere.

He knelt to one knee, and unsheathing the knife tucked in his boot, he used the small blade to cut a red rose from a bush at the base of its stem before presenting it to her.

She turned the flower around in her hands, her lips twitching with a smile. No magic aura lifted from the rose. Nothing powerful or special about it. It was just an ordinary rose.

But like the last time she mishandled a rose, she accidentally pricked herself on a thorn and hissed. "Ow! Why are these roses so dangerous?"

He laughed where he crouched, cupping his chin in his hand as he gave her an adorable grin. "It's red. Have you fallen madly in love with me yet?"

She lightly smacked his shoulder with the flower. "Oh, I think I fell a long time ago." Pulling him to his feet, she leaned in for another kiss to seal their love with a red rose between them. When they parted, joyful laughter erupted between them.

Rylan intertwined his fingers with hers, and together, they raced toward the unsolvable hedge maze, stopping before the very entrance that had doomed person after person to hours of headaches and frustration.

"Let's get lost for a while." His grip on her hand tightened, mischievous mirth shining in his eyes.

She returned his grin with one of her own. "My favorite thing to do."

ABOUT THE AUTHOR

Sydney Winward is an award-winning fantasy and paranormal romance author who dabbles in the occasional historical fiction. She loves building complex worlds filled with magic, strong characters, and emotional stories that can make you laugh and cry.

Sydney is the author of the Sunlight and Shadows Series and the best-selling Bloodborn Series, and when she's not writing, she's reading, thinking about stories, or going on adventures with her children. She lives in Utah with her husband and three amazing kids.

www.sydneywinward.com